D1425668

The Storytellers Two

Compiled by
Roger Mansfield

Illustrated by Brian Lee

SCHOFIELD & SIMS LTD HUDDERSFIELD

0 7217 0230 9
First printed 1971
Reprinted 1971
Reprinted 1972
Reprinted 1973
Reprinted 1974
Reprinted 1976
Reprinted 1977

ACKNOWLEDGMENTS

The author and publishers wish to thank the following for permission to use
copyright material:

Martin Secker & Warburg Ltd., for *Mummy to the Rescue* by Angus Wilson
from *Such Darling Dodos*.

Rosica Colin Ltd., for *The Disgrace of Jim Scarfedale* from *The Loneliness
of the Long Distance Runner* by Alan Sillitoe.

Mrs. Judith Wright McKinney, for her story *The Rabbiter*.

Curtis Brown Ltd., for *Breakfast* by John Steinbeck from *The Long Valley*,
and *A Sunrise on the Veld* by Doris Lessing from *This was the Old Chief's
Country*.

George G. Harrap & Co. Ltd., for *Late Night on Watling Street* by Bill
Naughton.

A. D. Peters & Company, for *The Murderer* by Ray Bradbury.
Reprinted by permission.

Printed in England by Henry Garnett and Company Limited, Rotherham and London.

Contents

Bill Naughton

Bill Naughton was born in County Mayo, Ireland in 1910, but not long afterwards his parents moved to England, to Bolton in Lancashire, where he lived for many years. After leaving school at fourteen, he took his first job, as an apprentice weaver in a local mill; later he worked as a coal-bagger and a lorry driver. In the years of the Depression when he was often 'on the dole', he spent the time in public libraries educating himself. Writing did not come easily to him but during the Second World War he began to produce short stories for magazines and by the end of the war he was successful enough to make his living by full-time writing. It was not until the late 1950's, however, that he became widely known, although he tries to avoid the publicity and 'most of the social carry-on' that accompany fame.

His childhood in Bolton and his experiences as a manual worker still provide much of the material for his stories; written in a lively, colloquial style, and concerned mainly with ordinary working class people, these display an unusual warmth and humour. They include: *The Goalkeeper's Revenge*, a collection of short stories 'for boys and about boys', from which 'Spit Nolan' (*Storytellers 1*) is taken; another collection, *Late Night on Watling Street*, the title story of which appears in *Storytellers 2*; and *One Small Boy*, a novel about a family who leave the west coast of Ireland to settle in Lancashire. He has also written several plays, the best known of which is probably *Alfie*—this was first a radio play and was then adapted as a stage play, a film and a novel. *Spring and Port Wine* and *All in Good Time* are another two plays which have been filmed (the latter as *The Family Way*).

Late Night on Watling Street

IT WAS after midnight when I drew my lorry on to the parking ground in front of 'Lew's' caff. I switched off the engine and lights, got out of the cab, knew it would be safe without locking it up, and stretched my limbs and looked up at the sky. It was all starry. The air had a nice fresh rinsed taste to it. I walked round the wagon and kicked my tyres, testing the ropes round my load, and with that nice week-end feeling you get on a Friday night, I went inside.

It was nearly empty. I went up to the counter. Ethel, Lew's young wife, was making a fresh pot of tea, and Lew was watching her. I heard him say, 'Make it any stronger an' you'll hatta serve it with knives and forks'.

'I can't stand the sight of weak tea,' said Ethel.

'You can get it a good colour without putting all that much in,' said Lew.

'It's not the colour a man wants,' said Ethel, 'it's body.' She winked at me. 'Eh, Bolton ?'

Lew hadn't seen me listening, and he tried to laugh it off. I didn't take much notice of him. I never do. He's turned fifty, has a thin face with red cheeks and sandy hair. He always wears a big jersey with a polo collar, a check cap, and sandals, and he always has a fag in his mouth. Box ? You could blow him over. But during the war, with all the shortage of food and fags, he suddenly found himself important, like most little shopkeepers and café owners, and he started giving orders, and took to wearing this boxer's rig-out. I hate fakes and show-offs, and Lew's one. But maybe he's not a bad bloke at heart, for they say he's good for a touch if you're short of cash. But I can never forget that he used to put soda in his tea urn, and I blame that for the guts-ache I used to get. That was before he married Ethel.

I said nothing to Ethel except to give her my usual warm nod and wink, and then I ordered a large tea, and asked could I have some egg and chips.

'Yes,' said Lew. 'She's got the chip pan all ready.'

'I'll bring your tea over,' said Ethel.

I knew he was getting at her over something. And I'd a good idea what it was—a driver called Jackson. Ethel wouldn't shut shop until he'd been. I said nothing because I reckoned I was lucky to get my egg and chips. Practically the only spot in the British Isles you could get them on a Friday night at that hour. I walked across to the big table where Taff and Ned were sitting, and sat at one end.

'I see old Babyface is out on the scout again,' said Taff.

'That dirty little blighter,' said Ned. 'I've known many a speed cop in my day, but never one like him, an' his mate. The way they creep up on your tail and hang there.'

'He's done that man Jackson three times,' said Taff.

'Once more,' said Ned, 'an' his licence will go for a walk for six months.'

Ethel brought my tea. She came up behind me and put it on the table. I saw her brown arm and strong woman's fingers.

Outside a lorry drew on to the parking ground and the engine revved up and then shut off. Taff said, 'That'll be Jackson.' I could see Lew looking a bit tense.

'It's not Jackson,' said Ethel. She smiled at me, and went back to the counter. The door opened and in came Walter, a driver from St. Helens, and behind him his trailer-mate, Willie.

Walter, a short little stiff chap, carrying his lunch basket, and Willie, one of these artistic lads you see around these days, with a silk scarf round his neck. He always followed Walter like a faithful poodle. Walter let out a shout and when he came up to Lew he got up on his toes and began boxing. This just suited Lew who began throwing in what he thought were snappy lefts. Old Walter could have let him have one and knocked him out for good. But he always liked to gee old Lew up a bit. He went up and kissed Ethel on the cheek.

'Love me as much as ever, love?' said Walter to Ethel.

'You know me, Walter,' said Ethel.

'That's why I'm asking,' said Walter.

It was a lively little entrance and it brightened the place up.

Taff called out, 'Did you see old Babyface on your way down?'

'Did we see him, Willie!' said Walter, 'Ethel, double egg and chips for my mate. I'm treating him.' Walter came over to the table and cocked his leg across a chair. 'We were just coming down the Long Hill there, we had the stick out, doing a nice forty-five, and old Willie here crooning away, when he suddenly broke off like he'd been shot. "What's up, Willie?" I says. "Sum'dy on our tail," says Willie. I revved up and put the old stick in and got into gear. I looked through the mirror. Not a thing in sight. I watched closely, not a thing. And I think the lad must be seeing something. I get the old speed down to a bit of a crawl, and still nothing in sight. "Are you sure, Willie?" I says. "I am that an' all," says Willie here. Well, I'm crawling along and still can't see nothing, and I comes to thinking that old Willie's psychic bump has let him down. So I tells him to lean out of the cab at his side while I give a chancy swerve and switch off my own lights for better seeing. Right enough it was that Babyface. Him and his mate had been stuck on our tail.'

'What happened then?' said Ned.

'They knew they'd been rumbled,' said Walter. 'So the next thing they drew ahead and went into a side road. And there they're stuck this minute, waiting for the next poor mug that comes down.'

Ethel came across with my egg and chips. A minute later she was back with Willie's.

'Ee, were you expecting me, Ethel?' said Willie, all smiles.

'Not *you*,' said Lew, looking at the door.

I was wiping my plate clean with bread when a lorry came belting off the road on to the parking ground outside. It hammered along and stopped with a loud brake squeal right at the door. Nobody looked up.

'That's Jackson now,' said Willie.

'And a good job his anchors are all right,' said Taff, 'or else——'

'Curse the man,' said Lew. 'He'll drive up to the blasted counter one of these fine days.' He turned what he must have thought was a tough face to the door. We all gave a look that way. It was Jackson all right. Lew quickly dropped his stare and started wiping a table.

'Has he got the rats in him?' said Ned.

'He's not in the best of moods surely,' said Taff.

Jackson came striding up slowly. He had a dark chin, pale face, black hair. As he was passing our table he saw Willie still eating his egg and chips. The sight of the plate seemed to stop him dead. His face went even darker. Willie looked dead nervous. Walter picked up the sauce bottle.

'Here y'are, Willie boy,' he said in a loud easy-going way, 'have a shake of the old bottle.'

Willie smiled at Walter. Jackson went to the next table, an empty one. When Lew saw that Walter had got one over Jackson, he seemed to take heart. He went up to the table. 'What is it?' he said.

'What's what?' said Jackson, looking for Ethel.

8

'Have you ordered ?' said Lew.

'Ordered ?' said Jackson. 'I'm not getting measured for a suit. Small tea.'

'That all ?' said Lew.

'That an' a bit of peace,' said Jackson.

'You're supposed to bring your own,' said Lew, walking away.

When he went up to the counter I could see he said something to Ethel, and I heard her say: 'There's times when your funny stuff isn't funny, Lew. I'll serve him.'

'You're welcome,' said Lew.

He looked hurt. She took his arm and smiled at him. He smiled back.

'Sorry,' said Ethel.

'We've had eighteen hours of it,' said Lew, looking at the clock. 'Another half-hour and we're through. What about a tune ?'

Ethel takes the tea across to Jackson. He gives one tight grip over her wrist.

'You want your egg an' chips, don't you Jack ?' she says.

Jackson shakes his head. Lew dropped his coin into the juke-box, and the next thing you can hear is a woman singing something about 'waltzing with her darling'. It's called 'The Tennessee Waltz'. Jackson kissed Ethel's arm. Then Ethel moved slowly away from his table, looking like a woman with a dream on her mind.

As it happens, old Lew is just moving away from the juke-box, and this music and woman's voice is filling the place, and Ethel comes up facing Lew with that faraway walk, and the next thing Lew has got hold of her and is dancing her gently around to a slow foxtrot or something.

Although I don't like him I had to admit to myself that he handled it nicely. And he danced nicely too, with a nice skilful movement. Then all began calling out, 'Life in the old dog yet', and 'Go on', but there was no doubt they all liked to see the dance. All except Jackson. His face went dead poisonous. He kept himself sitting there for a time and then he got to his feet. He went across to the juke-box, half turned his back on it, and gave it a back-heeler. It was a dead sharp kick, and the next thing there was a groan and the tune died away in the middle of the woman singing something about 'remembering the night'.

I looked up and saw old Lew's face. One second it had that look that comes over a chap's face when he's enjoying a dance. The next it had the look of a child that's had its dummy snatched out of its mouth in the middle of a good suck. Ethel gave Jackson a sharp sort of a look and went behind the counter. Willie looked towards Lew, his big eyes soft and wide open with sympathy. Lew stood there in a daze for a couple of ticks, then he went across to Jackson.

'You did that,' he said.

'What about it?' said Jackson.

'You'd no right,' said Lew. 'Didn't you see us dancin'?'

'I saw you,' said Jackson.

'I won't stand for it,' said Lew.

'What'll you do?' said Jackson.

'I'll show you what I'll do,' said Lew. Then he weakened. 'I mean, we were doin' no harm.'

'I told you I wanted some peace,' said Jackson. 'I've had enough din in my ears for the last five hours.'

'But you'd no right,' said Lew. He went across to the juke-box and shook it. You could hear the record whirring round but missing the needle or something. He came hurrying back to Jackson. 'You had no right to do what you did,' he said, talking legal like. 'I'd put my money in that box.'

Jackson leant back in his chair. 'Why didn't you say it was the money was troubling you?' he said. He put his hand in his pocket and drew out a fistful of silver and copper. 'Here y' are,' he said, holding out his hand. 'You can take it outa that.'

Lew, being a money-mean sort of bloke, couldn't help being caught off guard. The sight of money carelessly handled seems to make some people so that they can't think for a minute. He just stared at Jackson and at the money and didn't know what to do. Then Ethel came walking up behind Lew. She went round him in a gentle way, until she was facing Jackson, and before he knew what was happening she brought up her hand with a swift smack under his. The money went right up in the air and flew all over the place.

'And you,' she said, 'can take it out of that!'

Then she turned to Lew like a mother who has gone out into the street to help her lad who is being challenged by a bigger lad. 'Come on, Lew,' she said and led him back to the counter. We drivers said nothing. After all, Jackson himself was a driver. Jackson didn't know where to look or what to do. Then another lorry stopped outside.

The door opened with a quick jerk and in came Clive. A real spiv kid, the clothes, the walk, the lot, even to the old rub of the hands, as though he's going to sell you something. He comes whistling along.

'What you all bloomin' talkin' at once for?' he says, everything being dead silent. 'Large tea, Ethel, two of toast and drip. Don't be tight with the jelly—m'back's bad.'

Clive eyes everybody.

'Howzit goin', Bolton?' he says to me.

'Not bad,' I says.

Suddenly he makes a dive for something on the floor.

'Coo, I'm in bloomin' luck,' he says, picking up half a crown. I beckon with my thumb to where Jackson is sitting. Clive catches on. He goes across and puts it on the table in front of Jackson.

'I wouldn't rob you, Jackson,' he says. 'You might need it. I see old Babyface did you again—back up the road there on the Long Hill.'

As soon as Clive said that, the atmosphere changed.

'Ruddy hard luck, Jackson,' said Ned.

'I hope they don't scrub your licence,' said Taff.

I gave him a look. He didn't seem to have Babyface on his mind. A lot had happened to him since that.

'He must have nailed you just after he left us,' said Walter. He took out his fags, handed them round, hesitated, then held the packet out to Jackson. Jackson thought it over for a moment and then took one. The matey feeling came up then, the feeling of all being drivers and the law always after you.

Clive leant over the table and looked at Jackson. 'I was stuck in a lay-by up the road, mate when you came whamming past. You was goin' like the clappers of hell. *Whoof!* ...'

Ethel came up with Clive's tea and toast and drip.

'You was goin' at a hell of a lick, Jackson,' went on Clive. 'What was on your mind?'

Ethel was leaning over the table. I saw Jackson give her a long and hungry look. Ethel looked at him. She picked up his cup. 'Piece of my apple pie ?' she said. He nodded. Then he looked at Clive. 'What did you say ?' he said.

'Let it pass,' said Clive, his eyes following Ethel. He didn't miss much.

The atmosphere had come on matey, and even Lew came up and hung around.

'I wouldn't like to say what I'd do to a cop like that,' said Taff.

'Babyface ?' said Lew. 'Got his job to do, ain't he ? That's what he's paid for—bookin' you! Well, ain't it ?'

'He ain't paid bonus on the job,' said Ned. 'He don't have to creep on your tail. None of the others do it.'

'It's legal, ain't it ?' said Lew. 'You keep to the law too, then nob'dy can touch you.'

They went on yapping about the law then, about loads, log sheets, brakes, licences, and all the rest of it, with old Lew sticking his motty in at every chance.

Then Walter said, 'Has it ever struck you, Lew, what a dangerous caper it is—tailing a lorry ?'

I saw Jackson suddenly take an interest.

Clive said: 'Suppose you didn't know this geezer was on your tail ? Say you was doin' a nice fifty-five, when you spotted something just ahead of you ?'

'Yeh,' said Ned, 'an' down on the anchors.'

'Pull up with a jerk,' said Clive, 'and where's Babyface ?'

'Over the ruddy top,' said Taff.

'No, he ain't,' said Ned, 'he's *under* the back. You get out an' run round the back, and there's the bogey-men an' their car, practically buried under the back axle. "Wot wuz you-a-doin of ?" says Babyface. So you says, "Testin' my bloomin' brakes for efficiency. Why, officah, you've scratched your radiator—not to mention bashin' in your National 'Ealth dentures!" '

'Come on, Ned,' said Taff, rising, 'you'd talk all night.'

'It's about time you was all off,' said Lew. 'We want to get to bed.'

Ethel came over with Jackson's tea and apple pie. 'You go off, Lew,' she said. She looked at Jackson as she put the piece of pie in front of him, but he was staring down at the table. He didn't seem to notice the pie, or, come to that, Ethel herself.

'Can I trust you to lock up properly if I go off?' said Lew to Ethel.

'I'll help her,' said Walter.

'Then I think I'll go off to bed,' said Lew.

'That's right,' said Clive, 'let your brains cool down. "Keep to the law." Never heard such bull in all my life.'

'Come on, Taff,' said Ned.

They went off.

'I think I'll go,' said Lew.

'All right,' said Walter, 'go, but stop natterin' about it.'

'Don't be long, Ethel,' said Lew. 'Turf 'em out.'

'It's too late to hurry,' said Ethel.

'Good night, Lew,' said Willie.

'Good night, Willie lad,' said Lew.

When Lew had gone off, Clive turned to me: 'Fancy a game of darts, Lofthouse?'

They either call me by the town I come from or its best-known footballer.

'I'm getting down for ten minutes,' I said.

'I'll give you a game, Bermondsey,' said Walter.

They went off, up beside the counter for their darts game. I put my cap on the table and rested my forehead on it, and shut out all the light with my arms. Even if you don't sleep the eyes and head get rested. You need some relief when you've been driving a ten-tonner through the night. Ethel must have come up and sat at Jackson's table, because after a bit I could hear their voices.

'What made you blow your top?' he said.

'I won't stand by and see a young chap taking the micky out of an older one,' she said. 'I don't like you being that way, Jacky.'

'Before I forget,' said Jackson, 'I've something here for you. Hope they're not too squashed. I had to keep 'em out of sight.'

There was a bit of rustling and then Ethel whispered: 'Roses! how lovely, Jacky! Well, I never expected roses!'

Even with my head down I could smell roses.

Ethel must have given him a hand squeeze. He went on: 'Come off with me tonight. I'll wait for you outside in my tub. We'll drive off together. Don't worry about clothes—look, see, I've enough money in that book to buy you all the clothes you want.'

Post Office savings book. But I know how he felt. The thought of having a woman in the warm cab there beside you, as you drive through the night, is the most tempting thought a driver can get.

At least, that I can get. It's so cosy in the cab of your own lorry, with the faint warm smell of diesel oil, but it gets lonely. If only you had a woman beside you. For part of the time anyway.

Ethel went on about Lew: 'When I first came in that door,' I heard her say, 'I wasn't much to look at. I'd had things rough, I can tell you that, Jacky. And Lew is the first man I've ever met who has treated me with respect. He never tried anything on. And that's what I liked about him.'

'Am I trying anything on?' said Jackson. 'I'm asking you to come off with me.'

'And the day we got back after the marriage,' went on Ethel, 'he already had a new sign up outside. It said, "*Lew's and Ethel's*".'

'Come off it,' said Jackson. 'He made the ropiest cup of tea between here and Gretna Green. The place was fallin' apart, an' so was he. You've pulled it all together. You're straight with him.'

'Another thing Lew gave me,' said Ethel, 'was security.'

Jackson seemed to fly off the handle at that. 'Security? What the hell are you talking about! I come bashing down Watling Street tonight—never a perishing stop except to snatch your roses. One thought on my mind—will I see you? How do you think that rat Babyface caught me again?—and you talk to me about security.'

'Sorry, Jacky,' said Ethel. 'What happens if they take your licence?'

'No licence, no job,' said Jackson. 'But we'll see about that. They won't get me working under a roof that easily.'

Just then the juke-box let go 'The Tennessee Waltz' again. I looked up with a start, as though I'd been asleep. Willie was standing beside it. He called across to Walter, 'That's not the record I picked, Walter.' It was just then I looked towards Jackson. He looked real poisonous. He got up and walked slowly towards Willie at the juke-box.

'Jacky!' whispered Ethel. He took no notice.

Walter had spotted him. He left the darts game and hurried casually across to Willie beside the juke-box. Willie had seen Jackson, and he looked white.

'Enjoy yourself, lad,' said Walter. Then he turned and faced Jackson. I got up and walked across. Same as they used to say, Lancashire helps Lancashire. Walter was only a bantam; Jackson was on the big side and tough.

'Move over, Scouse,' said Jackson.

'What d'you want ?' said Walter.

'I'm going to stop that ruddy thing,' said Jackson.

'I don't think you are,' said Walter. His eyes never left Jackson as he handed the darts to Willie. I could see what Walter had in mind. He'd grab Jackson's coat lapels in a tick and pull him down and tup him with his head. And Jackson wouldn't be able to see for blood. I could almost hear the crack of Jackson's nose in my ears, even before it happened.

Ethel slipped round.

'What's up ?' she said.

'Willie's paid to hear a tune,' said Walter, 'and he's goin' to hear one.'

'Yeh, but it might not be the one he's paid for,' said Jackson.

Jackson had a savage look on his face. But Walter was determined, and on the aware.

'Don't make any trouble,' said Ethel. 'Please go, and let me lock up.'

Jackson turned and looked at her. Walter was ready to make his grab. I stepped in.

'Come on, Walt,' I said.

'Not till the tune's up,' he said.

So we all stood there for half a minute until the woman on the record stopped singing.

'You can all go now,' said Ethel.

'Ee, but we haven't paid yet, Ethel,' said Willie.

'Ee, lad, so you haven't,' said Ethel, taking him off a bit.

That seemed to break up the tension.

'What about the old darts?' said Clive.

Walter took the darts off Willie.

'Is it me?' he said.

'Yip,' said Clive. 'You want seventy-nine for game. Not be a minute, Ethel.'

Walter toed the line. He threw a nineteen, then a twenty, and a double-top with the last dart.

'Who'd 'ave bloomin' thought it!' said Clive, putting down his darts.

We all paid and walked to the door. 'Have you a minute, Bolton?' said Jackson. I nodded. He slipped back and had a last word with Ethel. I went up beside Walter.

'I was right there behind you, Walter,' I said, 'but I reckoned you didn't need me.'

Walter took off his cap and patted his head: 'I had this ready for him,' he said.

I went across to my tub. Then Jackson came up.

'I was going to ask you,' he said; 'you ain't got an old driving mirror, have you?'

As soon as he said it I remembered I had one in my tool-box. And it struck me that he must have seen it when I once lent him a spanner. He took out his fags and handed me one. Then he shone the torch in my tool-box. I got the driving mirror out. It was one that had been wrenched away when I drew too close to a wagon at the sidings one day. The metal arm had been ripped from the bracket.

'That do you?' I said.

'It might,' he said.

I didn't ask him what he wanted it for. If he wants me to know, I reckoned, he'll tell me.

'You've been done for speeding?' he said.

'More'n once,' I said.

'The cop who charges you has got to have a witness—that so ?' he said.

'His mate,' I said, 'that's all.'

'There's got to be two of 'em in court,' he said.

'If you plead "not guilty" an' make a case of it,' I said. 'But how many drivers do ? You know damn' well you're guilty.'

'But they've both got to be there,' he said. 'Haven't they ?'

'Look here, Jackson,' I said, 'if you're goin' on about Babyface doin' you tonight, forget it. You——'

'Look here,' cut in Jackson, 'if you want to question his witness and his witness fails to appear, or either one of them fails to appear——'

'Then it's "failure to produce witnesses",' I said, 'and you get "Case Dismissed".'

'That's what I wanted to know,' said Jackson.

'But I'll tell you one thing you're sufferin' from, Jackson,' I said, 'that's a bad dose of *copitis*.'

'You said it,' he said. 'I could murder the perishing lot of 'em.'

'It won't get you nowhere,' I said. 'We've all had it some time or other. Anyway, they won't take your licence just for speedin'.'

'It's not speedin'. He's doin' me for dangerous drivin'.' said Jackson.

'That's a bit more serious,' I said.

'An' not only that,' said Jackson.

'What else ?' I said.

'I'd a fiver folded up in my licence when I handed it over,' he said.

'A fiver! You must be crazy,' I said. 'It should be a quid. An' you get the licence back with a caution an' no quid. What's wrong with that ? I'd sooner give a cop a quid than a magistrate a fiver.'

'I'd sooner cut their throats,' said Jackson, 'the lot of 'em. Babyface is trying to make out I wanted to bribe him.'

'I suppose you said you kept it in your licence for safety?' I said.

Jackson nodded.

'Then,' I said, 'it's your word against his.'

'Against his and his mate's, and I know whose they'll take,' he said. Then he picked up the mirror and had a good look at it. 'We'll see,' he said. 'They ain't heard the charge yet. There's another three weeks to go. Anything could happen in that time.' He waved the mirror and went off.

It was a fortnight later, about two o'clock in the morning, a pitch black night, and I was belting along Watling Street, hoping I might make 'Lew's' in time. I was going at a fair lick, because you can see better on a dark night, since your headlights carve out the road for you, and you don't get those dicey shadows the moon makes. I had my eye watching out for Babyface, for I knew I was on his beat.

Suddenly, ahead down the road, I saw a lorry's headlights flashing on and off, giving me the danger signal. I flashed back, braked, and watched the road behind me and the road ahead. You can't be too careful on a trunk road at night.

I drew up in a safe clear spot. In the beam of my headlight I could see a lorry skew-whiff across the road. There was a black car that had crashed into the back of it with such force that it seemed to be buried under the chassis. I lit a fag. As I was getting out a driver came running up to me.

'Leave your headlights on, Bolton,' he called. 'They need all the light they can get.'

'That you, Ned?' I said. 'What's happened?'

'A right smash-up,' said Ned. He whispered: 'It's old Jackson. Police car run into the back of him. They're trying to get the bodies out.'

We walked down together to the smash-up. The police and ambulance men were on the job. They were trying to jack up the back axle of the lorry so that they could get the car out. The police car hooter was going all the time. The blue plate on the back of the car with the word 'POLICE' on it was intact, but that was about all that was. Nobody would ever drive that car again. As for the two blokes inside, well, one glimpse was enough.

'Babyface?' I said to Ned.

'It was,' said Ned. 'The poor blighter. His mate, too.' He gave me a knowing look, but said no more.

I heard someone talking in a husky voice and I turned and saw Jackson. He was talking to a young patrol cop who was making notes in his book.

'Well, I'll tell you all I know,' said Jackson. 'I'm coming along at a fair crack. No use wrapping it up, I had my toe down, because I wanted to get to the caff down the road before they close. I usually have egg and chips about this time. But I was keeping my eyes open and the road was dead clear in front of and behind me— so far as I could see. I could have sworn to it. And I was just coming along there, when on the bend here, dead in front of me, I saw what looked like a body curled in the roadway.'

'A body?' said the cop. 'Where is it now?'

'I looked after,' said Jackson. 'See—under there.'

He pointed under his lorry. We all looked.

'That old overcoat?' said the cop.

'I can see what it is *now*,' said Jackson. 'But catch it in your headlights an' it looks different.'

The cop nodded.

'I've known many an old geezer get drunk and go to sleep in the middle of the road,' went on Jackson. 'Anyway, I slammed on my brakes at once. Then I got the shock of my life. *Something hit me from behind*. I couldn't think what had happened. It wasn't a tap, it was a real bash. Even with my brakes on it knocked me across the road.'

The patrol cop looked sympathetic.

'What did you do then?' he asked.

'It took me a minute or two to come round,' said Jackson. 'The shock and one thing and another. Then I got out of the cab and walked round to the back. It's dark, see, and for a bit I couldn't make out what had happened. I could hear his horn blowing away in my ears, but I didn't know where it was coming from, not at first. Then suddenly I began to make it out. I looked inside the car and saw 'em. It was a shock, mate, I can tell you that. How are they? Will they be all right?'

'Take it easy,' said the cop. 'We're doing all we can.'

Jackson wiped his face with his hand: 'Is it all right if I walk down the road and get myself a cup of tea?' he asked. 'I feel all out.'

The cop said, 'Just a minute, I'll see.' He went up to a police sergeant and one of the ambulance men. Jackson turned and winked at me, then he went on wiping his forehead. The patrol cop came back and said, 'So long as you are not too far away.'

Jackson said, 'I'll be in the caff.'

'Better let me have your licence,' said the cop.

'I'll get it out of my coat pocket,' said Jackson, 'in the cab. He turned to me. 'You'll give me a lift down the road, Lofty?'

The cop warmed up: 'Come on,' he said, 'let's get the road clear, or we'll be having another smash-up. Tell the other drivers not to line up along there.'

Jackson got into my cab. I drove round by his lorry and down the road to 'Lew's'. He was thinking about something and he said nothing as we went down the road, and I didn't feel like talking either. When I drew up to a halt outside Lew's he turned to me and digging his hands inside his coat he carefully pulled something out.

' 'Ere you are, mate,' he said.

I looked. In his hand was the driving mirror I had lent him. The glass was broken.

'It came in handy,' he said.

I didn't say anything. He looked like a man at peace with himself.

'I had it planted down below the floorboards,' he said.

'Oh, aye?' I said.

I wasn't as surprised as I made it sound.

'It was there waiting for Babyface,' he said. 'I knew whenever he crept on my tail, even if he had all his lights out, I'd spot him down in that mirror. Half an hour ago I caught him creeping up behind me. Right, I thought to myself, I'll draw you on, Charlie. I stuck in the booster gear and put my toe down. They fell for it and crept right up behind me. I was coming down Long Hill and I knew the exact spot he'd overtake me, just near the bend at the bottom. So as we were drawing near to it I got every ounce I could out of the old tub. We were fair cracking along, I can tell you. *Right mate*, I thought, *you're trying to do me, but I'm going to do you instead*. So, I steeled myself for the shock, then I slammed both feet down at once and swung on the handbrake at the same time.'

Jackson scratched his nose: 'I've got some lovely anchors on the old wagon. They drew me up like that. They'd have had to be good drivers to stop that quick. They didn't have a chance. They crashed right clean in the back.'

I felt I needed a bit of fresh air after that lot, so I got out of the cab. Jackson got out at the other side and walked round to me.

'First thing I did, when I stopped,' he said, 'was to take that old mirror out and put the floorboard back straight. Breaking that mirror brought 'em bad luck all right. Then I took that old top-coat that I had specially for the job and planted it on the road under the lorry. It's not mine.

24

He followed me round as I kicked at my tyres, and tested my loading ropes.

'Well, here's your mirror, mate,' he said.

I could hardly bear to look at it, let alone take hold of it.

'If you don't want it, I can soon lose it for you,' said Jackson. He was back in a minute. 'Take a ruddy good detective to find it now,' he said.

'Jackson,' I said, 'what's the idea telling me all this?'

He smiled softly at me and then he said: 'A bloke don't want to walk around with a basinful of that on his mind. I know I'm safe with an old driver. Come on, let's see if Ethel has the egg and chips ready.'

I followed him. At the door he turned and said to me: 'Nothing I like better than getting one across the law. Y'know what it means for my dangerous drivin' charge?—*Case dismissed*.'

I went in after him. There were half a dozen drivers in. Walter and Willie, young Clive, a driver and his mate from Glasgow, and an old driver from Hull. They all gave nods and waves to me. But as for Jackson, not a word was spoken. Not a sign was made. You felt everything going dead quiet. Lew was wiping the tables and kept right away from where Jackson sat. Ethel was behind the counter and she never gave him so much as a glance. She looked across to me and waved her hand. Jackson looked at her, but she didn't seem to see him. I knew then the word had gone round. It doesn't take long. He might have got one across the law, but he hadn't got one across Watling Street. Nobody would split, but already, North and South, they were putting the poison in for him. Within a week, he'd be lucky to get a civil cup of tea anywhere along the A5. And I could see by the look on Jackson's face he knew one thing at least—no matter what the police found or didn't find—he'd never get anywhere with Ethel now. And his driving days on Watling Street were over.

BILL NAUGHTON

25

Doris Lessing

Doris Lessing was born in Persia in 1919. Shortly afterwards her father went to Rhodesia, and she was brought up on a large farm there; she attended school in Salisbury. In 1949 she arrived in England with a small son to care for, very little money, and the manuscript of her first novel, *The Grass is Singing*. This fortunately was accepted almost at once and was published in 1950. It was followed a year later by a collection of short stories entitled *This Was the Old Chief's Country*, from which both 'No Witchcraft for Sale' (*Storytellers 1*) and 'Sunrise on the Veld' (*Storytellers 2*) are taken. In these, as in most of her work, the plot is relatively unimportant. Instead she concentrates on capturing ordinary but nevertheless significant moments in a person's life.

Although she now resides in England, many of her stories are still set in South Africa or Rhodesia, where she lived for twenty-five years. In 1954 she was presented with the Somerset Maugham Award for the promise of her writing in general, and the high standard of her fourth book—*Five—Short Novels*—in particular. Another volume of short stories which received high praise was *The Habit of Loving* (1957).

A Sunrise on the Veld

EVERY night that winter he said aloud into the dark of the pillow: Half-past four! Half-past four! till he felt his brain had gripped the words and held them fast. Then he fell asleep at once, as if a shutter had fallen; and lay with his face turned to the clock so that he could see it first thing when he woke.

It was half-past four to the minute, every morning. Triumphantly pressing down the alarm knob of the clock, which the dark half of his mind had outwitted, remaining vigilant all night and counting the hours as he lay relaxed in sleep, he huddled down for a last warm moment under the clothes, playing with the idea of lying abed for this once only. But he played with it for the fun of knowing that it was a weakness that he could defeat without effort; just as he set the alarm each night for the delight of the moment when he awoke and stretched his limbs, feeling the muscles tighten, and thought: Even my brain—even that! I can control every part of myself.

Luxury of warm rested body, with the arms and legs and fingers waiting like soldiers for a word of command! Joy of knowing that the precious hours were given to sleep voluntarily! —for he had once stayed awake three nights running, to prove that he could, and then worked all day, refusing even to admit that he was tired; and now sleep seemed to him a servant to be commanded and refused.

The boy stretched his frame full-length, touching the wall at his head with his hands, and the bed foot with his toes; then he sprung out, like a fish leaping from water. And it was cold, cold.

He always dressed rapidly, so as to try and conserve his night-warmth till the sun rose two hours later; but by the time he had on his clothes his hands were numbed and he could scarcely hold his shoes. These he could not put on for fear of waking his parents, who never came to know how early he rose.

As soon as he stepped over the lintel, the flesh of his soles contracted on the chill earth, and his legs began to ache with cold. It was night: the stars were glittering, the trees standing black and still. He looked for signs of day, for the greying of the edge of a stone, or a lightening in the sky where the sun would rise, but there was nothing yet. Alert as an animal he crept past the dangerous window, standing poised with his hand on the sill for one proudly fastidious moment, looking in at the stuffy blackness of the room where his parents lay.

Feeling for the grass edge of the path with his toes, he reached inside another window further along the wall, where his gun had been set in readiness the night before. The steel was icy, and numbed fingers slipped along it, so that he had to hold it in the crook of his arm for safety. Then he tiptoed to the room where the dogs slept, and was fearful that they might have been tempted to go before him; but they were waiting, their haunches crouched in reluctance at the cold, but ears and swinging tails greeting the gun ecstatically. His warning undertone kept them secret and silent till the house was a hundred yards back: then they bolted off into the bush, yelping excitedly. The boy imagined his parents turning in their beds and muttering: Those dogs again! before they were dragged back in sleep; and he smiled scornfully. He always looked back over his shoulder at the house before he passed a wall of trees that shut it from sight. It looked so low and small, crouching there under a tall and brilliant sky. Then he turned his back on it, and on the frowsting sleepers, and forgot them.

He would have to hurry. Before the light grew strong he must be four miles away; and already a tint of green stood in the hollow of a leaf, and the air smelled of morning and the stars were dimming.

He slung the shoes over his shoulder, veld skoen that were crinkled and hard with the dews of a hundred mornings. They would be necessary when the ground became too hot to bear. Now he felt the chilled dust push up between his toes, and he let the muscles of his feet spread and settle into the shape of the earth; and he thought: I could walk a hundred miles on feet like these! I could walk all day and never tire!

He was walking swiftly through the dark tunnel of foliage that in daytime was a road. The dogs were invisibly ranging the lower travelways of the bush, and he heard them panting. Sometimes he felt a cold muzzle on his leg before they were off again, scouting for a trail to follow. They were not trained, but free-running companions of the hunt, who often tired of the long stalk before the final shots, and went off on their own pleasure. Soon he could see them, small and wild-looking in a wild strange light, now that the bush stood trembling on the verge of colour, waiting for the sun to paint earth and grass afresh.

The grass stood to his shoulders; and the trees were showering a faint silvery rain. He was soaked; his whole body was clenched in a steady shiver.

Once he bent to the road that was newly scored with animals' trails, and regretfully straightened, reminding himself that the pleasure of tracking must wait till another day.

He began to run along the edge of a field, noting jerkily how it was filmed over with fresh spiderweb, so that the long reaches of great black clods seemed netted in glistening grey. He was using the steady lope he had learned by watching the natives, the run that is a dropping of the weight of the body from one foot to the next in a slow balancing movement that never tires, nor shortens the breath; and he felt the blood pulsing down his legs and along his arms, and the exultation and pride of body mounted in him till he was shutting his teeth hard against a violent desire to shout his triumph.

Soon he had left the cultivated part of the farm. Behind him the bush was low and black. In front was a long vlei, acres of long pale grass that sent back a hollowing gleam of light to a satiny sky. Near him thick swathes of grass were bent with the weight of water, and diamond drops sparkled on each frond.

The first bird woke at his feet and at once a flock of them sprang into the air calling shrilly that day had come; and suddenly, behind him, the bush woke into song. and he could hear the guinea fowl calling far ahead of him. That meant they would now be sailing down from their trees into thick grass, and it was for them he had come: he was too late. But he did not mind. He forgot he had come to shoot. He set his legs wide, and balanced from foot to foot, and swung his gun up and down in both hands horizontally, in a kind of improvised exercise, and let his head sink back till it was pillowed in his neck muscles, and watched how above him small rosy clouds floated in a lake of gold.

Suddenly it all rose in him: it was unbearable. He leapt up into the air, shouting and yelling wild, unrecognisable noises. Then he began to run, not carefully as he had before, but madly, like a wild thing. He was clean crazy, yelling mad with the joy of living and a superfluity of youth. He rushed down that vlei under a tumult of crimson and gold, while all the birds of the world sang about him. He ran in great leaping strides, and shouted as he ran, feeling his body rise into the crisp rushing air and fall back surely on to sure feet; and thought briefly, not believing that such a thing could happen to him, that he could break his ankle any moment, in this thick tangled grass. He cleared bushes like a

duiker, leaped over rocks; and finally came to a dead stop at a place where the ground fell abruptly away below him to the river. It had been a two-mile-long dash through waist-high growth, and he was breathing hoarsely and could no longer sing. But he poised on a rock and looked down at stretches of water that gleamed through stooping trees, and thought suddenly, I am fifteen! Fifteen! The words came new to him; so that he kept repeating them wonderingly, with swelling excitement; and he felt the years of his life with his hands, as it were, as if he were counting marbles, each one hard and separate and compact, each one a wonderful shining thing. That was what he was; fifteen years of this rich soil, and this slow-moving water, and air that smelt like a challenge whether it was warm and sultry at noon, or as brisk as cold water, like it was now.

There was nothing he couldn't do, nothing! A vision came to him, as he stood there, like when a child hears the word 'eternity' and tries to understand it, and time takes possession of the mind. He felt his life ahead of him as a great and wonderful thing, something that was his; and he said aloud, with the blood rising to his head: all the great men of the world have been as I am now, and there is nothing I can't become, nothing I can't do; there is no country in the world I cannot make part of myself, if I choose. I contain the world. I can make of it what I want. If I choose, I can change everything that is going to happen: it depends on me, and what I decide now.

The urgency, and the truth and the courage of what his voice was saying exulted him so that he began to sing again, at the top of his voice, and the sound went echoing down the river gorge. He stopped for the echo, and sang again: stopped and shouted. That was what he was! he sang, if he chose; and the world had to answer him.

And for minutes he stood there, shouting and singing and waiting for the lovely eddying sound of the echo; so that his own new strong thoughts came back and washed round his head, as if someone were answering him and encouraging him; till the gorge was full of soft voices clashing back and forth from rock to rock over the river. And then it seemed as if there was a new voice. He listened, puzzled, for it was not his own. Soon he was leaning forward, all his nerves alert, quite still: somewhere close to him there was a noise that was no joyful bird, nor tinkle of falling water, nor ponderous movement of cattle.

There it was again. In the deep morning hush that held his future and his past, was a sound of pain, and repeated over and over: it was a kind of shortened scream, as if someone, something, had no breath to scream. He came to himself, looked about him, and called for the dogs. They did not appear: they had gone off on their own business, and he was alone. Now he was clean sober, all the madness gone. His heart beating fast, because of that frightened screaming, he stepped carefully off the rock and went towards a belt of trees. He was moving cautiously, for not so long ago he had seen a leopard in just this spot.

At the edge of the trees he stopped and peered, holding his gun ready; he advanced, looking steadily about him, his eyes narrowed. Then, all at once, in the middle of a step, he faltered, and his face was puzzled. He shook his head impatiently, as if he doubted his own sight.

There, between two trees, against a background of gaunt black rocks, was a figure from a dream, a strange beast that was horned and drunken-legged, but like something he had never even imagined. It seemed to be ragged. It looked like a small buck that had black ragged tufts of fur standing up irregularly all over it, with patches of raw flesh beneath . . . but the patches of rawness were disappearing under moving black and came again elsewhere; and all the time the creature screamed, in small gasping screams, and leaped drunkenly from side to side, as if it were blind.

33

Then the boy understood: it *was* a buck. He ran closer, and again stood still, stopped by a new fear. Around him the grass was whispering and alive. He looked wildly about, and then down. The ground was black with ants, great energetic ants that took no notice of him, but hurried and scurried towards that fighting shape, like glistening black water flowing through the grass.

And, as he drew in his breath and pity and terror seized him, the beast fell and the screaming stopped. Now he could hear nothing but one bird singing, and the sound of the rustling, whispering ants.

He peered over at the writhing blackness that jerked convulsively with the jerking nerves. It grew quieter. There were small twitches from the mass that still looked vaguely like the shape of a small animal.

It came into his mind that he should shoot it and end its pain; and he raised the gun. Then he lowered it again. The buck could no longer feel; its fighting was a mechanical protest of the nerves. But it was not that that made him put down the gun. It was a swelling feeling of rage and misery and protest that expressed itself in the thought: if I had not come it would have died like this: so why should I interfere? All over the bush things like this happen; they happen all the time; this is how life goes on, by living things dying in anguish. He gripped the gun between his knees and felt in his own limbs the myriad swarming pain of the twitching animal that could no longer feel, and set his teeth, and said over and over again under his breath: I can't stop it. I can't stop it. There is nothing I can do.

He was glad that the buck was unconscious and had gone past suffering so that he did not have to make a decision to kill it even when he was feeling with his whole body: this is what happens, this is how things work.

It was right—that was what he was feeling. *It was right and nothing could alter it.*

The knowledge of fatality, of what has to be, had gripped him and for the first time in his life; and he was left unable to make any movement of brain or body, except to say: 'Yes, yes. That is what living is.' It had entered his flesh and his bones and grown into the furthest corners of his brain and would never leave him. And at that moment he could not have performed the smallest action of mercy, knowing as he did, having lived on it all his life, the vast, unalterable, cruel veld, where at any moment one might stumble over a skull or crush the skeleton of some small creature.

Suffering, sick and angry, but also grimly satisfied with his new stoicism, he stood there leaning on his rifle, and watched the seething black mound grow smaller. At his feet, now, were ants trickling back with pink fragments in their mouths, and there was a fresh acid smell in his nostrils. He sternly controlled the uselessly convulsing muscles of his empty stomach, and reminded himself: the ants must eat too! At the same time he found that the tears were streaming down his face, and his clothes were soaked with the sweat of that other creature's pain.

The shape had grown small. Now it looked like nothing recognisable. He did not know how long it was before he saw the blackness thin, and bits of white showed through, shining in the sun—yes, there was the sun, just up, glowing over the rocks. Why, the whole thing could not have taken longer than a few minutes.

He began to swear, as if the shortness of the time was in itself unbearable, using the words he had heard his father say. He strode forward, crushing ants with each step, and brushing them off his clothes, till he stood above the skeleton, which lay sprawled under a small bush. It was clean picked. It might have been lying there years, save that on the white bone were pink fragments of gristle. About the bones ants were ebbing away, their pincers full of meat.

The boy looked at them, big black ugly insects. A few were standing and gazing up at him with small glittering eyes.

35

'Go away!' he said to the ants, very coldly. 'I am not for you—not just yet, at any rate. Go away.' And he fancied that the ants turned and went away.

He bent over the bones and touched the sockets in the skull; that was where the eyes were, he thought incredulously, remembering the liquid dark eyes of a buck. And then he bent the slim foreleg bone, swinging it horizontally in his palm.

That morning, perhaps an hour ago, this small creature had been stepping proud and free through the bush, feeling the chill on its hide even as he himself had done, exhilarated by it. Proudly stepping the earth, tossing its horns, frisking a pretty white tail, it had sniffed the cold morning air. Walking like kings and conquerors it had moved through this free-held bush, where each blade of grass grew for it alone, and where the river ran pure sparkling water for its slaking.

And then—what had happened? Such a swift surefooted thing could surely not be trapped by a swarm of ants?

The boy bent curiously to the skeleton. Then he saw that the back leg that lay uppermost and strained out in the tension of death, was snapped midway in the thigh, so that broken bones jutted over each other uselessly. So that was it! Limping into the ant-masses it could not escape, once it had sensed the danger. Yes, but how had the leg been broken? Had it fallen, perhaps? Impossible, a buck was too light and graceful. Had some jealous rival horned it?

What could possibly have happened? Perhaps some natives had thrown stones at it, as they do, trying to kill it for meat, and had broken its leg. Yes, that must be it.

Even as he imagined the crowd of running, shouting natives, and the flying stones, and the leaping buck, another picture came into his mind. He saw himself, on any one of these bright ringing mornings, drunk with excitement, taking a snapshot at some half-seen buck. He saw himself with the sun lowered, wondering whether he had missed or not; and thinking at last that it was late, and he wanted his breakfast, and it was not worthwhile to track miles after an animal that would very likely get away from him in any case.

For a moment he would not face it. He was a small boy again, kicking sulkily at the skeleton, hanging its head, refusing to accept the responsibility.

Then he straightened up, and looked down at the bones with an odd expression of dismay, all the anger gone out of him. His mind went quite empty: all around him he could see trickles of ants disappearing into the grass. The whispering noise was faint and dry, like the rustling of a cast snakeskin.

At last he picked up his gun and walked homewards. He was telling himself half defiantly that he wanted his breakfast. He was telling himself that it was getting very hot, much too hot to be out roaming the bush.

Really, he was tired. He walked heavily, not looking where he put his feet. When he came within sight of his home he stopped, knitting his brows. There was something he had to think out. The death of that small animal was a thing that concerned him, and he was by no means finished with it. It lay at the back of his mind uncomfortably.

Soon, the very next morning, he would get clear of everybody and go to the bush and think about it.

DORIS LESSING

Saki

Saki (Hector Hugh Munro) was born in Akyab, Burma in 1870. After the death of their mother, the children were sent to North Devon to live with their grandmother and two fearsome aunts. The upbringing dispensed by these aunts had a marked effect on Saki, and many of the characters and attitudes to be found in his stories can be traced back to this period. In 1893 he took up a post with the Police in Burma but his health could not stand the climate and he was forced to return to England. Here he soon established for himself a reputation as a political satirist and from 1902 to 1908 travelled widely as foreign correspondent for the *Morning Post*, after which he settled in London. When war broke out in 1914, he enlisted immediately in the army. He was twice offered a commission but on both occasions refused it. Shortly before his death on 14 November, 1916, he was promoted to corporal.

Saki was also a novelist and a playright but his reputation rests mainly on his six volumes of short stories, all written between 1904 and 1914. Most of the stories are very short and provide maliciously amusing pictures of the prosperous middle classes in Edwardian England; a number, however, have a more macabre flavour to them. 'The Lumber Room' (*Storytellers 1*) is a comparatively gentle example of the way in which he poked fun at the pompous and hypocritical. 'Sredni Vashtar' (*Storytellers 2*) combines satire with an uncanny grimness. Both the women in these stories were modelled on his own fearsome Aunt Augusta: 'Aunt Augusta was an autocrat and had to be obeyed. She is more or less depicted in 'Sredni Vashtar' but the aunt in 'The Lumber Room' is herself to the life. Both aunts were guilty of mental cruelty and we often longed for revenge . . . '—Saki's stories, many of which have an unexpected twist at the end, are available in a number of anthologies and various omnibus editions.

Sredni Vashtar

CONRADIN was ten years old, and the doctor had pronounced his professional opinion that the boy would not live another five years. The doctor was silky and effete, and counted for little, but his opinion was endorsed by Mrs. De Ropp, who counted for nearly everything. Mrs. De Ropp was Conradin's cousin and guardian, and in his eyes she represented those three-fifths of the world that are necessary and disagreeable and real; the other two-fifths, in perpetual antagonism to the foregoing, were summoned up in himself and his imagination. One of these days Conradin supposed he would succumb to the mastering pressure of wearisome necessary things—such as illnesses and coddling restrictions and drawn-out dullness. Without his imagination, which was rampant under the spur of loneliness, he would have succumbed long ago.

Mrs. De Ropp would never, in her honestest moments, have confessed to herself that she disliked Conradin, though she might have been dimly aware that thwarting him 'for his good' was a duty which she did not find particularly irksome. Conradin hated her with a desperate sincerity which he was perfectly able to mask. Such few pleasures as he could contrive for himself gained an added relish from the likelihood that they would be displeasing to his guardian, and from the realm of his imagination she was locked out—an unclean thing, which should find no entrance.

In the dull, cheerless garden, overlooked by so many windows that were ready to open with a message not to do this or that, or a reminder that medicines were due, he found little attraction. The few fruit-trees that it contained were set jealously apart from his plucking, as though they were rare specimens of their kind blooming in an arid waste; it would probably have been difficult to find a market-gardener who would have offered ten shillings for their entire yearly produce. In a forgotten corner, however, almost hidden behind a dismal shrubbery, was a disused tool-shed of respectable proportions, and within its walls Conradin found a haven, something that took on the varying aspects of a playroom and a cathedral. He had peopled it with a legion of familiar phantoms, evoked partly from fragments of history and partly from his own brain, but it also boasted two inmates of flesh and blood. In one corner lived a ragged-plumaged Houdan hen, on which the boy lavished an affection that had scarcely another outlet. Further back in the gloom stood a large hutch, divided into two compartments, one of which was fronted with close iron bars. This was the abode of a large polecat-ferret, which a friendly butcher-boy had once smuggled, cage and all, into its present quarters, in exchange for a long-secreted hoard of small silver. Conradin was dreadfully afraid of the lithe, sharp-fanged beast, but it was his most treasured possession. Its very presence in the tool-shed was a secret and fearful joy, to be kept scrupulously from the knowledge of the Woman, as he privately dubbed his cousin. And one day, out of Heaven knows what material, he spun the beast a wonderful name, and from that moment it grew into a god and a religion. The Woman indulged in religion once a week at a church near by, and took Conradin with her, but to him the church service was an alien rite in the House of Rimmon. Every Thursday, in the dim and musty silence of the tool-shed, he worshipped with mystic and elaborate ceremonial before the wooden hutch where dwelt Sredni Vashtar, the great ferret. Red flowers in their season and scarlet berries in the winter-time were offered at his shrine, for he was a god who laid some special stress on the fierce

impatient side of things, as opposed to the Woman's religion, which, as far as Conradin could observe, went to great lengths in the contrary direction. And on great festivals powdered nutmeg was strewn in front of his hutch, an important feature of the offering being that the nutmeg had to be stolen. These festivals were of irregular occurrence, and were chiefly appointed to celebrate some passing event. On one occasion, when Mrs. De Ropp suffered from acute toothache for three days, Conradin kept up the festival during the entire three days, and almost succeeded in persuading himself that Sredni Vashtar was personally responsible for the toothache. If the malady had lasted for another day the supply of nutmeg would have given out.

The Houdan hen was never drawn into the cult of Sredni Vashtar. Conradin had long ago settled that she was an Anabaptist. He did not pretend to have the remotest knowledge as to what an Anabaptist was, but he privately hoped that it was dashing and not very respectable. Mrs. De Ropp was the ground plan on which he based and detested all respectability.

After a while Conradin's absorption in the tool-shed began to attract the notice of his guardian. 'It is not good for him to be pottering down there in all weathers,' she promptly decided, and at breakfast one morning she announced that the Houdan hen had been sold and taken away overnight. With her short-sighted eyes she peered at Conradin, waiting for an outbreak of rage and sorrow, which she was ready to rebuke with a flow of excellent precepts and reasoning. But Conradin said nothing: there was nothing to be said. Something perhaps in his white set face gave her a momentary qualm, for at tea that afternoon there was toast on the table, a delicacy which she usually banned on the ground that it was bad for him; also because the making of it 'gave trouble', a deadly offence in the middle-class feminine eye.

'I thought you liked toast,' she exclaimed, with an injured air, observing that he did not touch it.

'Sometimes,' said Conradin.

In the shed that evening there was an innovation in the worship of the hutch-god. Conradin had been wont to chant his praises, tonight he asked a boon.

'Do one thing for me, Sredni Vashtar.'

The thing was not specified. As Sredni Vashtar was a god he must be supposed to know. And choking back a sob as he looked at that other empty corner, Conradin went back to the world he so hated.

And every night, in the welcome darkness of his bedroom, and every evening in the dusk of the tool-shed, Conradin's bitter litany went up: 'Do one thing for me, Sredni Vashtar.'

Mrs. De Ropp noticed that the visits to the shed did not cease, and one day she made a further journey of inspection.

'What are you keeping in that locked hutch?' she asked. 'I believe it's guinea-pigs. I'll have them all cleared away.'

Conradin shut his lips tight, but the Woman ransacked his bedroom till she found the carefully hidden key, and forthwith marched down to the shed to complete her discovery. It was a cold afternoon, and Conradin had been bidden to keep to the house. From the furthest window of the dining-room the door of the shed could just be seen beyond the corner of the shrubbery, and there Conradin stationed himself. He saw the Woman enter, and then he imagined her opening the door of the sacred hutch and peering down with her short-sighted eyes into the thick straw bed where his god lay hidden. Perhaps she would prod at the straw in her clumsy impatience. And Conradin fervently breathed his prayer for the last time. But he knew as he prayed that he did not believe. He knew that the Woman would come out presently with that pursed smile he loathed so well on her face, and that in an hour or two the gardener would carry away his wonderful god, a god no longer, but a simple brown ferret in a hutch. And he knew that the Woman would triumph always as she triumphed now, and that he would grow ever more sickly under her pestering and domineering and superior wisdom, till one day nothing would matter much more with him, and the doctor would be proved right. And in the sting and misery of his defeat, he began to chant loudly and defiantly the hymn of his threatened idol:

Sredni Vashtar went forth,

His thoughts were red thoughts and his teeth were white.

His enemies called for peace, but he brought them death.

Sredni Vashtar the Beautiful.

And then of a sudden he stopped his chanting and drew closer to the window-pane. The door of the shed still stood ajar as it had been left, and the minutes were slipping by. They were long minutes, but they slipped by nevertheless. He watched the starlings running and flying in little parties across the lawn: he counted them over and over again, with one eye always on that swinging door. A sour-faced maid came in to lay the table for tea,

and still Conradin stood and waited and watched. Hope had crept by inches into his heart, and now a look of triumph began to blaze in his eyes that had only known the wistful patience of defeat. Under his breath, with a furtive exultation, he began once again the paean of victory and devastation. And presently his eyes were rewarded; out through that doorway came a long, low, yellow-and-brown beast, with eyes a-blink at the waning daylight, and dark wet stains around the fur of jaws and throat. Conradin dropped on his knees. The great polecat-ferret made its way down to a small brook at the foot of the garden, drank for a moment, then crossed a little plank bridge and was lost to sight in the bushes. Such was the passing of Sredni Vashtar.

'Tea is ready,' said the sour-faced maid; 'where is the mistress?'

'She went down to the shed some time ago,' said Conradin.

And while the maid went to summon her mistress to tea, Conradin fished a toasting-fork out of the sideboard drawer and proceeded to toast himself a piece of bread. And during the toasting of it and the buttering of it with much butter and the slow enjoyment of eating it, Conradin listened to the noises and silences which fell in quick spasms beyond the dining room door. The loud foolish screaming of the maid, the answering chorus of wondering ejaculations from the kitchen region, the scuttering footsteps and hurried embassies for outside help, and, then, after a lull, the scared sobbings and the shuffling tread of those who bore a heavy burden into the house.

'Whoever will break it to the poor child? I couldn't for the life of me!' exclaimed a shrill voice. And while they debated the matter among themselves, Conradin made himself another piece of toast.

SAKI

45

Stephen Crane

Stephen Crane was born in Newark in the State of New Jersey, U.S.A., on 1 November, 1871. He was the fourteenth child of a clerical family. His father, a Methodist minister, died in 1880, but Stephen's strict upbringing was continued just as rigorously by his mother. He spent a short time at university and then became a newspaper reporter in New York. His first novel, *Maggie: A Girl of the Streets* (1893), was printed at his own expense and was a commercial failure. The next, *The Red Badge of Courage*, appeared initially as a serial in a newspaper and was published as a book the following year, 1895. Like 'A Mystery of Heroism' (*Storytellers 1*), it dealt with the American Civil War. The same basic theme also occurs in both stories: under the stress of battle an ordinary soldier develops, without intending to do so, into a hero—a hero, however, who is real, who knows the meaning of fear, and who realises something of the truth about himself. This concern with the bravery of ordinary men shows itself again in 'The Veteran' (*Storytellers 2*).

The Red Badge of Courage was widely acclaimed and at the age of twenty-four Stephen Crane became a literary celebrity. Although he had, in fact, never been involved in a war when he wrote this novel, he became much sought after as a war correspondent because of the realistic atmosphere he was able to evoke. His experiences as a reporter in the Spanish-American and Graeco-Turkish wars provided him with material for several other books. But the American public, although continuing to admire his stories, came to disapprove of his 'dissolute' way of life. It was perhaps partly to escape their censure that he moved to England, where he spent his last years near Rye in Sussex. He died in the Black Forest in June, 1900.

The Veteran

OUT of the low window could be seen three hickory trees placed irregularly in a meadow that was resplendent in springtime green. Farther away, the old, dismal belfry of the village church loomed over the pines. A horse meditating in the shade of one of the hickories lazily swished his tail. The warm sunshine made an oblong of vivid yellow on the floor of the grocery.

'Could you see the whites of their eyes?' said the man who was seated on a soap-box.

'Nothing of the kind,' replied old Henry warmly. 'Just a lot of flitting figures, and I let go at where they 'peared to be the thickest. Bang!'

'Mr. Fleming,' said the grocer—his deferential voice expressed somehow the old man's exact social weight—'Mr. Fleming, you never was frightened much in them battles, was you?'

The veteran looked down and grinned. Observing his manner, the entire group tittered. 'Well, I guess I was,' he answered finally. 'Pretty well scared, sometimes. Why, in my first battle I thought the sky was falling down. I thought the world was coming to an end. You bet I was scared.'

Every one laughed. Perhaps it seemed strange and rather wonderful to them that a man should admit the thing, and in the tone of their laughter there was probably more admiration than if old Fleming had declared that he had always been a lion. Moreover, they knew that he had ranked as an orderly sergeant, and so their opinion of his heroism was fixed. None, to be sure, knew how an orderly sergeant ranked, but then it was understood to be somewhere just shy of a major-general's stars. So when old Henry admitted that he had been frightened, there was a laugh.

'The trouble was,' said the old man, 'I thought they were all shooting at me. Yes, sir, I thought every man in the other army was aiming at me in particular, and only me. And it seemed so darned unreasonable, you know. I wanted to explain to 'em what an almighty good fellow I was, because I thought then they might quit all trying to hit me. But I couldn't explain and they kept on being unreasonable—blim!—blam!—bang! So I run!'

Two little triangles of wrinkles appeared at the corners of his eyes. Evidently he appreciated some comedy in this recital. Down near his feet, however, little Jim, his grandson, was visibly horror-stricken. His hands were clasped nervously, and his eyes

were wide with astonishment at this terrible scandal, his most magnificent grandfather telling such a thing.

'That was at Chancellorsville. Of course, afterward I got kind of used to it. A man does. Lots of men, though, seem to feel all right from the start. I did, as soon as I "got on to it," as they say now; but at first I was pretty flustered. Now, there was young Jim Conklin, old Si Conklin's son—that used to keep the tannery —you none of you recollect him—well, he went into it from the start just as if he was born to it. But with me it was different. I had to get used to it.'

When little Jim walked with his grandfather he was in the habit of skipping along on the stone pavement in front of the three stores and the hotel of the town and betting that he could avoid the cracks. But upon this day he walked soberly, with his hand gripping two of his grandfather's fingers. Sometimes he kicked abstractedly at dandelions that curved over the walk. Any one could see that he was much troubled.

'There's Sickles's colt over in the medder, Jimmie,' said the old man. 'Don't you wish you owned one like him?'

'Um,' said the boy, with a strange lack of interest. He continued his reflections. Then finally he ventured: 'Grandpa—now—was that true what you was telling those men?'

'What?' asked the grandfather. 'What was I telling them?'

'Oh, about your running.'

'Why, yes, that was true enough, Jimmie. It was my first fight, and there was an awful lot of noise, you know.'

Jimmie seemed dazed that this idol, of its own will, should so totter. His stout boyish idealism was injured.

Presently the grandfather said: 'Sickles's colt is going for a drink. Don't you wish you owned Sickles's colt, Jimmie?'

The boy merely answered: 'He ain't as nice as our'n.' He lapsed then into another moody silence.

One of the hired men, a Swede, desired to drive to the county-seat for purposes of his own. The old man loaned a horse and an unwashed buggy. It appeared later that one of the purposes of the Swede was to get drunk.

After quelling some boisterous frolic of the farm-hands and boys in the garret, the old man had that night gone peacefully to sleep, when he was aroused by clamouring at the kitchen door. He grabbed his trousers, and they waved out behind as he dashed forward. He could hear the voice of the Swede, screaming and blubbering. He pushed the wooden button, and, as the door flew open, the Swede, a maniac, stumbled inward, chattering, weeping, still screaming. 'De barn fire! Fire! Fire! De barn fire! Fire! Fire! Fire!'

There was a swift and indescribable change in the old man. His face ceased instantly to be a face; it became a mask, a grey thing, with horror written about the mouth and eyes. He hoarsely shouted at the foot of the little rickety stairs, and immediately, it seemed, there came down an avalanche of men. No one knew that during this time the old lady had been standing in her nightclothes at the bedroom door, yelling: 'What's th' matter? What's th' matter? What's th' matter?'

When they dashed toward the barn it presented to their eyes its usual appearance, solemn, rather mystic in the black night. The Swede's lantern was overturned at a point some yards in front of the barn doors. It contained a wild little conflagration of its own, and even in their excitement some of those who ran felt a gentle secondary vibration of the thrifty part of their minds at sight of this overturned lantern. Under ordinary circumstances it would have been a calamity.

But the cattle in the barn were trampling, trampling, trampling, and above this noise could be heard a humming like the song of innumerable bees. The old man hurled aside the great doors, and a yellow flame leaped out at one corner and sped and wavered frantically up the old grey wall. It was glad, terrible, this single flame, like the wild banner of deadly and triumphant foes.

The motley crowd from the garret had come with all the pails of the farm. They flung themselves upon the well. It was a leisurely old machine, long dwelling in indolence. It was in the habit of giving out water with a sort of reluctance. The men stormed at it, cursed it; but it continued to allow the buckets to be filled only after the wheezy windlass had howled many protests at the mad-handed men.

With his opened knife in his hand old Fleming himself had gone headlong into the barn, where the stifling smoke swirled with the air-currents, and where could be heard in its fullness the terrible chorus of the flames, laden with tones of hate and death, a hymn of wonderful ferocity.

He flung a blanket over an old mare's head, cut the halter close to the manger, led the mare to the door, and fairly kicked her out to safety. He returned with the same blanket, and rescued one of the workhorses. He took five horses out, and then came out him-

self, with his clothes bravely on fire. He had no whiskers, and very little hair on his head. They soused five pailfuls of water on him. His eldest son made a clean miss with the sixth pailful, because the old man had turned and was running down the decline and around to the basement of the barn, where were the stanchions of the cows. Some one noticed at the time that he ran very lamely, as if one of the frenzied horses had smashed his hip.

The cows, with their heads held in the heavy stanchions, had thrown themselves, strangled themselves, tangled themselves: done everything which the ingenuity of their exuberant fear could suggest to them.

Here, as at the well, the same thing happened to every man save one. Their hands went mad. They became incapable of everything save the power to rush into dangerous situations.

The old man released the cow nearest the door, and she, blind drunk with terror, crashed into the Swede. The Swede had been running to and fro babbling. He carried an empty milk-pail, to which he clung with an unconscious, fierce enthusiasm. He shrieked like one lost as he went under the cow's hoofs, and the milk-pail, rolling across the floor, made a flash of silver in the gloom.

Old Fleming took a fork, beat off the cow, and dragged the paralyzed Swede to the open air. When they had rescued all the cows save one, which had so fastened herself that she could not be moved an inch, they returned to the front of the barn and stood sadly, breathing like men who had reached the final point of human effort.

Many people had come running. Someone had even gone to the church, and now, from the distance, rang the tocsin note of the old bell. There was a long flare of crimson on the sky, which made remote people speculate as to the whereabouts of the fire.

The long flames sang their drumming chorus in voices of the heaviest bass. The wind whirled clouds of smoke and cinders into

the faces of the spectators. The form of the old barn was outlined in black amid these masses of orange-hued flames.

And then came this Swede again, crying as one who is the weapon of the sinister fates. 'De colts! De colts! You have forgot de colts!'

Old Fleming staggered. It was true; they had forgotten the two colts in the box-stalls at the back of the barn. 'Boys', he said, 'I must try to get 'em out.' They clamoured about him then, afraid for him, afraid of what they should see. Then they talked wildly each to each. 'Why, it's sure death!' 'He would never get out.' 'Why, it's suicide for a man to go in there!' Old Fleming stood absent-mindedly at the open doors. 'The poor little things,' he said. He rushed into the barn.

When the roof fell in, a great funnel of smoke swarmed toward the sky, as if the old man's mighty spirit, released from its body —a little bottle—had swelled like the genie of fable. The smoke was tinted rose-hue from the flames, and perhaps the unutterable midnights of the universe will have no power to daunt the colour of this soul. STEPHEN CRANE

Judith Wright

Judith Wright (Mrs. J. McKinney) was born in Australia, near Armidale, New South Wales, in 1915. She spent much of her early girlhood in the outback and, because there were no schools nearby, received her first education through the N.S.W. Correspondence School. Then, after attending the New England Girls' School, she went to Sydney University. This was followed by a year in Europe. When she returned to Australia, she worked as a stenographer, a secretary, a statistician and an agriculturalist. She now lives with her husband at Mount Tamborine in Southern Queensland.

She is best known for her poetry, being recognised as one of the most outstanding poets writing in English today, and certainly Australia's leading contributor. Her first book of poems, *The Moving Image*, was published in 1946; since then she has written several more and has also edited *The Oxford Book of Australian Verse*. Her short stories, however, are not written in what is commonly thought of as a 'poetic' style: there are no involved descriptions or exaggerated images; instead the prose is clear and economic. Her poet's understanding is revealed more by her deep feeling for Australian life, both in the suburbs and in the country, as shown by 'In the Park' (*Storytellers 1*) and 'The Rabbiter' (*Storytellers 2*) respectively. Her dialogue, for example, has an authentic Australian tone, without relying on a multitude of idioms to create the effect. She has published only one volume of short stories, *The Nature of Love* (1966). Her other work includes literary criticism, four books for children and a biographical novel.

The Rabbiter

'OH, YES, he's a decent young fellow, that,' said Leda's father, talking with his mouth full, but in a tone more melancholy than usual. 'I knew his father well. He was in my platoon; died later, but I knew him well. I'll give this young chap work, since he wants it; there's nothing but the rabbiting, but he can have the three top paddocks. They'll give him a living for the winter, if he keeps at it. I don't know what he thinks he's doing ... no sense, at that age, any of them ... however, he'll learn, and it's his own business. And he's a decent young fellow.'

Leda, in a dream, watched the movements of his moustache as it rose and fell to enclose mouthfuls of stew. The three top paddocks? She had wanted to trap there, herself, this winter. There was one big black rabbit and a yellow one, and she wanted the skins to make slippers. One black fur slipper, one yellow one. 'Dad,' she wanted to ask, 'may I go up and try to get a couple of rabbits before he moves into the top paddocks?' But her father did not approve of her trapping; girls did not do such things.

'I'll ask the trapper, when he comes,' she thought. She would promise to give him all she caught, except just the black and yellow rabbits. Those belonged to her. She had seen them feeding round the warren near the rock outcrop in Top Weaner Paddock; she had been saving them up for winter, when the fur grew long and glossy and the trapping season began. She could have got them long ago, so they belonged to her.

The rabbiter came in an old blue utility truck, so old that it sagged down on one side further and further until it almost tilted to the ground, and then he had to get out and jump up and down on the running-board until it righted itself. The back of it was piled up with traps and a tattered tent and canvas stretcher. Leda watched the truck as the rabbiter pulled up at the house, for directions from her father.

But there was someone else inside it; someone who stayed still, so still that Leda did not see her until the wind blew aside a corner of the canvas side-curtain. Then she knew it was Willow—Willow Green from the river camp. Leda had not seen her for years; the people of Mannima did not encourage the river-camp people around.

'Dad,' she said afterwards, 'why did the rabbiter have Willow Green in his truck?'

Her father looked melancholy again and played with his moustache. 'She's his wife, Leda; he's married her, they say. What on earth he thought he was doing—however, that's his business. But she'll be back at the camp in a year or maybe less—a half-caste gipsy! But I knew his father; knew the man well. And he's a decent young fellow enough.'

Leda felt somehow brought to a standstill. She waited around for days, wondering whether, now, she could go up and ask the rabbiter about those two rabbits. It was a new situation, and she did not feel sure whether a married rabbiter would agree to let her trap in his country. But the thought that perhaps he had seen them already, he was already working on their warren, was too much to bear at last. She went up one day to Top Weaner Paddock and tied her pony to a tree.

The tent was pitched in the shelter of a big rock near an old bloodwood tree. From the branches of the tree hung the wire frames on which the drying skins were stretched, inside-out and all in one piece, like a leather jacket. Leda looked carefully from a distance at the colour of the fur which edged each skin, but neither the yellow nor the black rabbit had been caught as yet. The tent was quiet, but a remnant of fire smoked outside, under a blackened billy hung between a couple of forked saplings.

It was early morning, but the rabbiter, Leda thought, should be back from his trap-round by now and skinning the catch at the tent. She was uncertain what to do, for she could see nobody, until at last she caught a glimpse of him over the gully, near the rocky outcrop where her rabbits lived. She made down into the gully at once.

The rabbiter was stooping over something on the ground. He looked up at once as Leda's head rose over the gully-edge, and recognised her. 'It's a possum,' he said, as though he knew what she was wondering.

Leda looked down at the trapped possum on the ground. It was young and frightened, but its leg was broken and it could not get away.

'Get a straight stick, will you?' said the man. 'I'll hold it here.'

Leda looked at him. 'I don't want it killed.'

'A straight stick,' the rabbiter repeated. 'For a splint, see?'

'Oh,' said Leda. She searched under the trees, and came back with a smooth twig. The rabbiter pulled a piece of string from his pocket, but Leda shook her head and tore up her handkerchief, which was old and not very clean. The man splinted the leg, while Leda held the writhing possum down with her foot.

'Now we'll have to look after it, I s'pose,' the rabbiter said. He looked doubtfully at the young possum. 'We haven't got the right food for it.'

'I'll take it home,' Leda said, 'and look after it for you. If you'll let me do one thing.' She explained about the rabbits.

'I've seen the black one,' said the rabbiter. 'All right, you can have them if you want. But what'll you do with the possum when its leg's healed up? They're a nuisance to have about.'

'I'll bring it back up here and let it go,' said Leda. 'It'll find its way back to the others. Possums and wild things are better in their own places. Houses don't suit them.'

'No, that's right,' said the rabbiter. He wrapped the possum in a spoiled rabbit-skin, so that it could not use its claws, and gave it to Leda. 'Now I'd better go up and get on with the skinning. The dogs are hungry.' His four dogs waited with savage smiles for the rabbit-carcases.

'I've brought my traps,' Leda said. 'Can I set them? I know where the black one likes to play in the evenings.'

She set her traps and carried the possum up the slope to her pony. Willow Green did not come out of the tent, but Leda saw her watching.

After that Leda rode up to Top Weaner Paddock every morning before breakfast. Her father was easily put off with a tale of practising for the show hurdles, over the logs in Top Ewe Paddock.

She called at the tent punctiliously every morning to hand over the rabbits she had caught; the black and the yellow were hard to trap. The rabbiter talked to her easily, but Willow seldom spoke; she hung her head, dropped her round black eyes and drew with a bare foot in the dust round the tent. She was beautiful, Leda thought. Half-castes were beautiful and gipsies were beautiful, and Willow was best of all the people from the river-camp. Leda did not mind her not talking; she knew Willow felt friendly.

At last she caught the yellow rabbit. It was a doe, but without kittens—a beautiful skin marked with white and black. She had seen the black rabbit again, and knew it was a buck, big and cunning. She showed Willow and the rabbiter the skin, and they admired it.

'You might get the buck easy now,' the rabbiter said. 'They might be mates. He might go wander around looking for her, and

forget about the traps. They do that sometimes, even the knowing ones.'

Leda shook her head doubtfully. 'Dad says they don't mate with each other, the odd-coloured ones. They mate with the ordinary rabbits. I suppose it's so the young ones will be ordinary-coloured and not too conspicuous. It's too easy to see the odd-coloured ones; the hawks and foxes get them easier.'

Willow drew a rabbit in the dust with her toe. She looked thoughtful.

Leda's possum was nearly healed now. It was beginning to scramble round the house at night, trying to get into cupboards; once it knocked down a jam-jar and Leda's mother complained. But it was not strong enough yet to have the splint taken off.

When Leda rode up one day, the rabbiter was busy stringing frames on the fence-wires to dry. He had a lot of skins now, nearly a truck-load, and the dogs were fat and sated with rabbit-flesh so that they scarcely troubled to chase such rabbits as remained in the warrens. He looked at Leda sadly.

'Got to take the skins to town this week. Willow wants to see her mother and the rest, and we got a truck-load nearly. I guess this paddock's about cleaned out.'

'Are you moving over into Top Ram Paddock when you come back?' Leda asked.

'Well, yes and no,' the rabbiter said. He was quieter than usual. 'I mean, I don't know. Willow don't like it here.'

'Why not?'

'Too lonely, she reckons. She isn't used to being on her own too much. Natural, I suppose.'

Leda thought of the river-camp, its crowded tin huts and broken-down caravans and tents, the dark people who laughed and quarrelled together and scattered out of the way when the white people passed. There was a kind of warmth about that place, a life that Leda had wondered about; something you didn't find with white people.

'But what are you going to do for a job?'

'I dunno,' said the rabbiter. 'I promised your father to clean out these paddocks. I dunno what to do. I'll try to get her to come back for the rest of the winter.'

'She couldn't go back and live in the camp, now,' Leda said, thinking this out. '*You* don't want to live there.'

The rabbiter made no reply.

'Perhaps she'd be happier if she was near your own family,' Leda suggested. 'It might be more like home for her.'

The rabbiter shook his head. 'It wouldn't be. My Mum and the rest don't want her.'

'Why not?' Leda said, shocked. Then she remembered what her father had said. 'Is it because she's coloured?'

The rabbiter nodded, ashamed. 'Oh, and while I think of it,' he said, 'that black buck was in one of my traps this morning. I left him for you to skin. Thought you might want it done some special way.'

'Oh, good,' Leda said. 'Then I can take my traps home. I'll just go and see Willow a minute.'

Willow was lying on a blue blanket on the bunk in the tent. The morning light through the yellowed canvas gave her skin a golden lustre as though she were made of some smooth flawless metal. 'Hullo,' she said listlessly, swinging one leg over the edge of the bunk.

'I've got that black buck now, so I don't need to come up again. I'm taking back the traps. I came in to say I mightn't be up again for a while; there's a new governess coming.'

Willow's huge dark eyes were blank and downcast. 'Well, goodbye.'

Leda hesitated. It was no good saying anything to Willow because you never knew what she thought. Then she went on down the slope, skinned her rabbit, packed the skin and the traps on her saddle and rode home. Neither the rabbiter nor Willow answered her goodbye wave.

The new governess was hard to get away from. Leda saw the blue truck come back a few days later, and saw that Willow was in it, but she did not have time to go back to the top paddocks. Winter was at its depth now; in the mornings the frost was hard on the ground, and her stable-fed pony was frisky and difficult to catch, and in the evenings it was dark almost before lesson-time ended. She made the rabbit-skins into two beautiful moccasins, with the skins tanned and dyed red for the outside and the fur inside, yellow for the left foot and black for the right. The possum was well now, and far too lively.

After her mother had complained a few more times, Leda took advantage of a Saturday afternoon to pack the possum securely in her saddle-bag and ride up to Top Weaner Paddock, to let him go in the place he had come from.

She met the blue truck driving down the track from Top Ram. The rabbiter pulled up and leaned out. He was tense and angry-looking.

'Seen Willow?' he asked.

Leda shook her head blankly.

'She's shot-through,' he said. 'Must have gone while I was out on the round. Don't tell anyone, though. I'll get her back.'

'I suppose she's gone in to the river-camp,' said Leda.

'Course she has,' said the rabbiter angrily. 'Twenty-miles to walk, and she didn't even wear her shoes. Might as well be a bloody myall and be done with it. I'll give her a good hiding when I catch her.' He crashed in the gears and drove off.

Leda rode on to Top Weaner and let the possum go. He went up a tree as though he recognised it, and vanished with a harsh spitting sound. Leda rode home.

When six days had passed and the rabbiter had not come back, her father began to grumble. The carcases piled up for burning in

Top Ram Paddock were beginning to smell, and the dogs had scattered them everywhere and were roaming loose. They would be at the sheep next.

Leda thought the matter over and then told him what the rabbiter had said.

'Poor bloke,' her father said with satisfaction. 'I don't know why he didn't know better than to take it on. I said she'd be back at the camp by the end of a year, and it hasn't taken three months. He's learning. But I wish he'd come back and collect those damn dogs.'

He never came back, and in the end her father shot the dogs and burned the tattered tent, which was blowing into ribbons with every westerly wind. Willow Green was back at the river-camp, and when Leda passed there one day Willow waved and smiled, but did not come over.

Leda never saw the possum again, either, though she sometimes stopped at the trees in Top Weaner Paddock and put a slice of bread underneath one of them.

JUDITH WRIGHT

Jack London

Jack London was born in America in San Francisco in 1876. He came from a poor working class family and was largely self-educated. Before becoming a writer, he was a sailor, gold miner and hobo. In the early 1900's he came to be regarded as 'the popular historian of the Klondike' and even today he is still remembered mainly for such stories as *The Call of the Wild* and *White Fang*—two vividly told tales of animal life in the Frozen North. Much of his work, however, expressed his strong socialist beliefs: *The Iron Heel*, a grimly prophetic novel about the future of civilisation, is perhaps the best known example of this aspect of his work. In virtually all his writing—whether it was about men or animals, set in Alaska or the South Seas, providing an exciting narrative or grim social criticism—there was a savage, brutal streak, an obsession with survival and destruction. This can be seen in both 'Bâtard' (*Storytellers 1*) and 'Love of Life' (*Storytellers 2*).

London, himself, seemed strangely bent on self-destruction. Although he earned as much as $75,000 a year, his financial affairs were invariably in chaos. He spent his money recklessly—on a lavish ranch in California, on an ill-fated world cruise in his own yacht, on a new castle called 'Wolf House' which burned to the ground six weeks before completion. Disillusioned with life, he began drinking heavily, although he continued to produce as many as four books a year in his desperate attempts to make even more money. He died, sick in body and mind, in November, 1916.

Love of Life

This out of all will remain—
They have lived and have tossed:
So much of the game will be gain,
Though the gold of the dice has been lost.

THEY limped painfully down the bank, and once the foremost of the two men staggered among the rough-strewn rocks. They were tired and weak, and their faces had the drawn expression of patience which comes of hardship long endured. They were heavily burdened with blanket packs which were strapped to their shoulders. Head-straps, passing across the forehead, helped support these packs. Each man carried a rifle. They walked in a stooped posture, the shoulders well forward, the head still farther forward, the eyes bent upon the ground.

'I wish we had just about two of them cartridges that's layin' in that cache of ourn,' said the second man.

His voice was utterly and drearily expressionless. He spoke without enthusiasm; and the first man, limping into the milky stream that foamed over the rocks, vouchsafed no reply.

The other man followed at his heels. They did not remove their footgear, though the water was icy cold—so cold that their ankles ached and their feet went numb. In places the water dashed against their knees, and both men staggered for footing.

The man who followed slipped on a smooth boulder, nearly fell, but recovered himself with a violent effort, at the same time uttering a sharp exclamation of pain. He seemed faint and dizzy and put out his free hand while he reeled, as though seeking support against the air. When he had steadied himself he stepped forward, but reeled again and nearly fell. Then he stood still and looked at the other man, who had never turned his head.

The man stood still for fully a minute, as though debating with himself. Then he called out:

'I say, Bill, I've sprained my ankle.'

Bill staggered on through the milky water. He did not look around. The man watched him go, and though his face was expressionless as ever, his eyes were like the eyes of a wounded deer.

The other man limped up the farther bank and continued straight on without looking back. The man in the stream watched him. His lips trembled a little, so that the rough thatch of brown hair which covered them was visibly agitated. His tongue even strayed out to moisten them.

'Bill!' he cried out.

It was the pleading cry of a strong man in distress, but Bill's head did not turn. The man watched him go, limping grotesquely and lurching forward with stammering gait up the slow slope toward the soft sky line of the low-lying hill. He watched him go till he passed over the crest and disappeared. Then he turned his gaze and slowly took in the circle of the world that remained to him now that Bill was gone.

Near the horizon the sun was smouldering dimly, almost obscured by formless mists and vapours, which gave an impression of mass and density without outline or tangibility. The man pulled out his watch, the while resting his weight on one leg. It was four o'clock, and as the season was near the last of July or first of August—he did not know the precise date within a week or two —he knew that the sun roughly marked the northwest. He looked to the south and knew that somewhere beyond those bleak hills lay the Great Bear Lake; also, he knew that in that direction the

Arctic Circle cut its forbidding way across the Canadian Barrens. This stream in which he stood was a feeder to the Coppermine River, which in turn flowed north and emptied into Coronation Gulf and the Arctic Ocean. He had never been there, but he had seen it, once, on a Hudson Bay Company chart.

Again his gaze completed the circle of the world about him. It was not a heartening spectacle. Everywhere was soft sky line. The hills were all low lying. There were no trees, no shrubs, no grasses —naught but a tremendous and terrible desolation that sent fear swiftly dawning into his eyes.

'Bill!' he whispered, once and twice, 'Bill!'

He cowered in the midst of the milky water, as though the vastness were pressing in upon him with overwhelming force, brutally crushing him with its complacent awfulness. He began to shake as with an ague fit, till the gun fell from his hand with a splash. This served to rouse him. He fought with his fear and pulled himself together, groping in the water and recovering the weapon. He hitched his pack farther over on his left shoulder, so as to take a portion of its weight from off the injured ankle. Then he proceeded, slowly and carefully, wincing with pain, to the bank.

He did not stop. With a desperation that was madness, un-mindful of the pain, he hurried up the slope to the crest of the hill over which his comrade had disappeared—more grotesque and comical by far than that limping, jerking comrade. But at the crest he saw a shallow valley, empty of life. He fought with his fear again, overcame it, hitched the pack still farther over on his left shoulder, and lurched on down the slope.

The bottom of the valley was soggy with water, which the thick moss held, spongelike, close to the surface. This water squirted out from under his feet at every step, and each time he lifted a foot the action culminated in a sucking sound as the wet moss reluctantly released its grip. He picked his way from muskeg to muskeg, and followed the other man's footsteps along and across the rocky ledges which thrust like islets through the sea of moss.

Though alone, he was not lost. Farther on he knew he would come to where dead spruce and fir, very small and weazened, bordered the shore of a little lake, the *titchin-nichilie*, in the tongue of the country, the 'land of little sticks'. And into that lake flowed a small stream, the water of which was not milky. There was rush grass on that stream—this he remembered well—but no timber, and he would follow it till its first trickle ceased at a divide. He would cross this divide to the first trickle of another stream, flowing to the west, which he would follow until it emptied into the River Dease, and here he would find a cache under an upturned canoe and piled over with many rocks. And in this cache would be ammunition for his empty gun, fishhooks and lines, a small net—all the utilities for the killing and snaring of food. Also, he would find flour—not much—a piece of bacon, and some beans.

Bill would be waiting for him there, and they would paddle away south down the Dease to the Great Bear Lake. And south across the lake they would go, ever south, till they gained the Mackenzie. And south, still south, they would go, while the winter raced vainly after them, and the ice formed in the eddies, and the days grew chill and crisp, south to some warm Hudson Bay Company post, where timber grew tall and generous and there was grub without end.

These were the thoughts of the man as he strove onward. But hard as he strove with his body, he strove equally hard with his mind, trying to think that Bill had not deserted him, that Bill would surely wait for him at the cache. He was compelled to think this thought, or else there would not be any use to strive, and he would have lain down and died. And as the dim ball of the sun sank slowly into the northwest he covered every inch—and many times—of his and Bill's flight south before the downcoming winter. And he conned the grub of the cache and the grub of the Hudson Bay Company post over and over again. He had not eaten for two days; for a far longer time he had not had all he wanted to eat. Often he stooped and picked pale muskeg berries, put them into his mouth, and chewed and swallowed them. A muskeg berry is a bit of seed enclosed in a bit of water. In the mouth the water melts away and the seed chews sharp and bitter. The man knew there was no nourishment in the berries, but he chewed them patiently with a hope greater than knowledge and defying experience.

At nine o'clock he stubbed his toe on a rocky ledge, and from sheer weariness and weakness staggered and fell. He lay for some time, without movement, on his side. Then he slipped out of the pack straps and clumsily dragged himself into a sitting posture. It was not yet dark, and in the lingering twilight he groped about among the rocks for shreds of dry moss. When he had gathered a heap he built a fire—a smouldering, smudgy fire—and put a tin pot of water on to boil.

He unwrapped his pack and the first thing he did was to count his matches. There were sixty-seven. He counted them three times to make sure. He divided them into several portions, wrapping them in oil paper, disposing of one bunch in his empty tobacco pouch, of another bunch in the inside band of his battered hat, of a third bunch under his shirt on the chest. This accomplished, a panic came upon him, and he unwrapped them all and counted them again. There were still sixty-seven.

He dried his wet footgear by the fire. The moccasins were in soggy shreds. The blanket socks were worn through in places, and his feet were raw and bleeding. His ankle was throbbing, and he gave it an examination. It had swollen to the size of his knee. He tore a long strip from one of his two blankets and bound the ankle tightly. He tore other strips and bound them about his feet to serve for both moccasins and socks. Then he drank the pot of water, steaming hot, wound his watch, and crawled between his blankets.

He slept like a dead man. The brief darkness around midnight came and went. The sun arose in the northeast—at least the day dawned in that quarter, for the sun was hidden by grey clouds.

At six o'clock he awoke, quietly lying on his back. He gazed straight up into the grey sky and knew that he was hungry. As he rolled over on his elbow he was startled by a loud snort, and saw a bull caribou regarding him with alert curiosity. The animal was not more than fifty feet away, and instantly into the man's mind leaped the vision and the savour of a caribou steak sizzling and frying over a fire. Mechanically he reached for the empty gun, drew a bead, and pulled the trigger. The bull snorted and leaped away, his hoofs rattling and clattering as he fled across the ledges.

The man cursed and flung the empty gun from him. He groaned aloud as he started to drag himself to his feet. It was a slow and arduous task. His joints were like rusty hinges. They worked harshly in their sockets, with much friction, and each bending or unbending was accomplished only through a sheer exertion of will. When he finally gained his feet, another minute or so was consumed in straightening up, so that he could stand erect as a man should stand.

He crawled up a small knoll and surveyed the prospect. There were no trees, no bushes, nothing but a grey sea of moss scarcely diversified by grey rocks, grey lakelets, and grey streamlets. The sky was grey. There was no sun nor hint of sun. He had no idea of north, and he had forgotten the way he had come to this spot the night before. But he was not lost. He knew that. Soon he would come to the land of the little sticks. He felt that it lay off to the left somewhere, not far—possibly just over the next low hill.

He went back to put his pack into shape for travelling. He assured himself of the existence of his three separate parcels of matches, though he did not stop to count them. But he did linger,

debating, over a squat moose-hide sack. It was not large. He could hide it under his two hands. He knew that it weighed fifteen pounds—as much as all the rest of the pack—and it worried him. He finally set it to one side and proceeded to roll the pack. He paused to gaze at the squat moose-hide sack. He picked it up hastily with a defiant glance about him, as though the desolation were trying to rob him of it; and when he rose to his feet to stagger on into the day, it was included in the pack on his back.

He bore away to the left, stopping now and again to eat muskeg berries. His ankle had stiffened, his limp was more pronounced, but the pain of it was as nothing compared with the pain of his stomach. The hunger pangs were sharp. They gnawed and gnawed until he could not keep his mind steady on the course he must pursue to gain the land of little sticks. The muskeg berries did not allay this gnawing, while they made his tongue and the roof of his mouth sore with their irritating bite.

He came upon a valley where rock ptarmigan rose on whirring wings from the ledges and muskegs. Ker—ker—ker was the cry they made. He threw stones at them, but could not hit them. He placed his pack on the ground and stalked them as a cat stalks a sparrow. The sharp rocks cut through his pants legs till his knees left a trail of blood; but the hurt was lost in the hurt of his hunger. He squirmed over the wet moss, saturating his clothes and chilling his body; but he was not aware of it, so great was his fever for food. And always the ptarmigan rose, whirring, before him, till their ker—ker—ker became a mock to him, and he cursed them and cried aloud at them with their own cry.

Once he crawled upon one that must have been asleep. He did not see it until it shot up in his face from its rocky nook. He made a clutch as startled as was the rise of the ptarmigan, and there remained in his hand three tail feathers. As he watched its flight he hated it, as though it had done him some terrible wrong. Then he returned and shouldered his pack.

As the day wore along he came into valleys or swales where game was more plentiful. A band of caribou passed by, twenty and odd animals, tantalizingly within rifle range. He felt a wild desire to run after them, a certitude that he could run them down. A black fox came toward him, carrying a ptarmigan in his mouth. The man shouted. It was a fearful cry, but the fox, leaping away in fright, did not drop the ptarmigan.

Late in the afternoon he followed a stream, milky with lime, which ran through sparse patches of rush grass. Grasping these rushes firmly near the root, he pulled up what resembled a young onion sprout no larger than a shingle nail. It was tender, and his teeth sank into it with a crunch that promised deliciously of food. But its fibres were tough. It was composed of stringy filaments saturated with water, like the berries, and devoid of nourishment. He threw off his pack and went into the rush grass on hands and knees, crunching and munching, like some bovine creature.

He was very weary and often wished to rest, to lie down and sleep; but he was continually driven on, not so much by his desire to gain the land of little sticks as by his hunger. He searched little ponds for frogs and dug up the earth with his nails for worms, though he knew in spite that neither frogs nor worms existed so far north.

He looked into every pool of water vainly until, as the long twilight came on, he discovered a solitary fish, the size of a minnow, in such a pool. He plunged his arm in up to the shoulder, but it eluded him. He reached for it with both hands and stirred up the milky mud at the bottom. In his excitement he fell in, wetting himself to the waist. Then the water was too muddy to admit of his seeing the fish, and he was compelled to wait until the sediment had settled.

The pursuit was renewed, till the water was again muddied. But he could not wait. He unstrapped the tin bucket and began to bail the pool. He bailed wildly at first, splashing himself and flinging the water so short a distance that it ran back into the pool. He worked more carefully, striving to be cool, though his heart was pounding against his chest and his hands were trembling. At the end of half an hour the pool was nearly dry. Not a cupful of water remained. And there was no fish. He found a hidden crevice among the stones through which it had escaped to the adjoining and larger pool—a pool which he could not empty in a night and a day. Had he known of the crevice, he could have closed it with a rock at the beginning and the fish would have been his.

Thus he thought, and crumpled up and sank down upon the wet earth. At first he cried softly to himself, then he cried loudly to the pitiless desolation that ringed him around; and for a long time after he was shaken by great dry sobs.

He built a fire and warmed himself by drinking quarts of hot water, and made camp on a rocky ledge in the same fashion he had the night before. The last thing he did was to see that his matches were dry and to wind his watch. The blankets were wet and clammy. His ankle pulsed with pain. But he knew only that he was hungry, and through his restless sleep he dreamed of feasts and banquets and of food served and spread in all imaginable ways.

He awoke chilled and sick. There was no sun. The grey of earth and sky had become deeper, more profound. A raw wind was blowing, and the first flurries of snow were whitening the hilltops. The air about him thickened and grew white while he made a fire and boiled more water. It was wet snow, half rain, and the flakes were large and soggy. At first they melted as soon as they came in contact with the earth, but ever more fell, covering the ground, putting out the fire, spoiling his supply of moss fuel.

This was a signal for him to strap on his pack and stumble onward, he knew not where. He was not concerned with the land of little sticks, nor with Bill and the cache under the upturned canoe by the River Dease. He was mastered by the verb 'to eat'. He was hunger-mad. He took no heed of the course he pursued, so long as

75

that course led him through the swale bottoms. He felt his way through the wet snow to the watery muskeg berries, and went by feel as he pulled up the rush grass by the roots. But it was tasteless stuff and did not satisfy. He found a weed that tasted sour and he ate all he could find of it, which was not much, for it was a creeping growth, easily hidden under the several inches of snow.

He had no fire that night, nor hot water, and crawled under his blanket to sleep the broken hunger-sleep. The snow turned into a cold rain. He awakened many times to feel it falling on his upturned face. Day came—a grey day and no sun. It had ceased raining. The keenness of his hunger had departed. Sensibility, as far as concerned the yearning for food, had been exhausted. There was a dull, heavy ache in his stomach, but it did not bother him so much. He was more rational, and once more he was chiefly interested in the land of little sticks and the cache by the River Dease.

He ripped the remnant of one of his blankets into strips and bound his bleeding feet. Also, he recinched the injured ankle and prepared himself for a day of travel. When he came to his pack, he paused long over the squat moose-hide sack, but in the end it went with him.

The snow had melted under the rain, and only the hilltops showed white. The sun came out, and he succeeded in locating the points of the compass, though he knew now that he was lost. Perhaps, in his previous day's wanderings, he had edged away too far to the left. He now bore off to the right to counteract the possible deviation from his true course.

Though the hunger pangs were no longer so exquisite, he realised that he was weak. He was compelled to pause for frequent rests, when he attacked the muskeg berries and rush-grass patches. His tongue felt dry and large, as though covered with a fine hairy growth, and it tasted bitter in his mouth. His heart gave him a great deal of trouble. When he had travelled a few minutes it would begin a remorseless thump, thump, thump, and then leap up and away in a painful flutter of beats that choked him and made him go faint and dizzy.

In the middle of the day he found two minnows in a large pool. It was impossible to bail it, but he was calmer now and managed to catch them in his tin bucket. They were no longer than his little finger, but he was not particularly hungry. The dull ache in his stomach had been growing duller and fainter. It seemed almost that his stomach was dozing. He ate the fish raw, masticating with painstaking care, for the eating was an act of pure reason. While he had no desire to eat, he knew that he must eat to live.

In the evening he caught three more minnows, eating two and saving the third for breakfast. The sun had dried stray shreds of moss, and he was able to warm himself with hot water. He had not covered more than ten miles that day; and the next day, travelling whenever his heart permitted him, he covered no more than five miles. But his stomach did not give him the slightest uneasiness. It had gone to sleep. He was in a strange country, too, and the caribou were growing more plentiful, also the wolves. Often their yelps drifted across the desolation, and once he saw three of them slinking away before his path.

Another night; and in the morning, being more rational, he untied the leather string that fastened the squat moose-hide sack. From its open mouth poured a yellow stream of coarse gold dust and nuggets. He roughly divided the gold in halves, caching one half on a prominent ledge, wrapped in a piece of blanket, and returning the other half to the sack. He also began to use strips of the one remaining blanket for his feet. He still clung to his gun, for there were cartridges in that cache by the River Dease.

This was a day of fog, and this day hunger awoke in him again. He was very weak and was afflicted with a giddiness which at times blinded him. It was no uncommon thing now for him to stumble and fall; and stumbling once, he fell squarely into a ptarmigan nest. There were four newly hatched chicks, a day old —little specks of pulsating life no more than a mouthful; and he ate them ravenously, thrusting them alive into his mouth and crunching them like eggshells between his teeth. The mother ptarmigan beat about him with great outcry. He used his gun as a club with which to knock her over, but she dodged out of reach. He threw stones at her and with one chance shot broke a wing. Then she fluttered away, running, trailing the broken wing, with him in pursuit.

The little chicks had no more than whetted his appetite. He hopped and bobbed clumsily along on his injured ankle, throwing stones and screaming hoarsely at times; at other times hopping and bobbing silently along, picking himself up grimly and patiently when he fell, or rubbing his eyes with his hand when the giddiness threatened to overpower him.

The chase led him across swampy ground in the bottom of the valley, and he came upon footprints in the soggy moss. They were not his own—he could see that. They must be Bill's. But he could not stop, for the mother ptarmigan was running on. He would catch her first, then he would return and investigate.

He exhausted the mother ptarmigan; but he exhausted himself. She lay panting on her side. He lay panting on his side, a dozen feet away, unable to crawl to her. And as he recovered she recovered, fluttering out of reach as his hungry hand went out to her. The chase was resumed. Night settled down and she escaped. He stumbled from weakness and pitched head foremost on his face, cutting his cheek, his pack upon his back. He did not move for a long while; then he rolled over on his side, wound his watch, and lay there until morning.

Another day of fog. Half of his last blanket had gone into foot wrappings. He failed to pick up Bill's trail. It did not matter. His hunger was driving him too compellingly—only—only he wondered if Bill, too, were lost. By midday the irk of his pack became too oppressive. Again he divided the gold, this time merely spilling half of it on the ground. In the afternoon he threw the rest of it away, there remaining to him only the half blanket, the tin bucket, and the rifle.

An hallucination began to trouble him. He felt confident that one cartridge remained to him. It was in the chamber of the rifle and he had overlooked it. On the other hand, he knew all the time that the chamber was empty. But the hallucination persisted. He fought it off for hours, then threw his rifle open and was confronted with emptiness. The disappointment was as bitter as though he had really expected to find the cartridge.

He plodded on for half an hour, when the hallucination arose again. Again he fought it, and still it persisted, till for very relief he opened his rifle to unconvince himself. At times his mind wandered farther afield, and he plodded on, a mere automaton, strange conceits and whimsicalities gnawing at his brain like worms. But these excursions out of the real were of brief duration, for ever the pangs of the hunger-bite called him back. He was jerked back abruptly once from such an excursion by a sight that caused him nearly to faint. He reeled and swayed, doddering like a drunken man to keep from falling. Before him stood a horse. A horse! He could not believe his eyes. A thick mist was in them, intershot with sparkling points of light. He rubbed his eyes savagely to clear his vision, and beheld, not a horse, but a great brown bear. The animal was studying him with bellicose curiosity.

The man had brought his gun halfway to his shoulder before he realised. He lowered it and drew his hunting knife from its beaded sheath at his hip. Before him was meat and life. He ran his thumb along the edge of his knife. It was sharp. The point was sharp. He would fling himself upon the bear and kill it. But his heart began its warning thump, thump, thump. Then followed the wild upward leap and tattoo of flutters, the pressing as of an

79

iron band about his forehead, the creeping of the dizziness into his brain.

His desperate courage was evicted by a great surge of fear. In his weakness, what if the animal attacked him? He drew himself up to his most imposing stature, gripping the knife and staring hard at the bear. The bear advanced clumsily a couple of steps, reared up, and gave vent to a tentative growl. If the man ran, he would run after him; but the man did not run. He was animated now with the courage of fear. He, too, growled, savagely, terribly, voicing the fear that is to life germane and that lies twisted about life's deepest roots.

The bear edged away to one side, growling menacingly, himself appalled by this mysterious creature that appeared upright and unafraid. But the man did not move. He stood like a statue till the danger was past, when he yielded to a fit of trembling and sank down into the wet moss.

He pulled himself together and went on, afraid now in a new way. It was not the fear that he should die passively from lack of food, but that he should be destroyed violently before starvation had exhausted the last particle of the endeavour in him that made toward surviving. There were the wolves. Back and forth across the desolation drifted their howls, weaving the very air into a fabric of menace that was so tangible that he found himself, arms in the air, pressing it back from him as it might be the walls of a wind-blown tent.

Now and again the wolves, in packs of two and three, crossed his path. But they sheered clear of him. They were not in sufficient numbers, and besides they were hunting the caribou, which did not battle, while this strange creature that walked erect might scratch and bite.

In the late afternoon he came upon scattered bones where the wolves had made a kill. The debris had been a caribou calf an hour before, squawking and running and very much alive. He contemplated the bones, clean-picked and polished, pink with the cell life in them which had not yet died. Could it possibly be that he might be that ere the day was done! Such was life, eh? A vain and fleeting thing. It was only life that pained. There was no hurt in death. To die was to sleep. It meant cessation, rest. Then why was he not content to die?

But he did not moralise long. He was squatting in the moss, a bone in his mouth, sucking at the shreds of life that still dyed it faintly pink. The sweet meaty taste, thin and elusive almost as a memory, maddened him. He closed his jaws on the bones and crunched. Sometimes it was the bone that broke, sometimes his teeth. Then he crushed the bones between rocks, pounded them to a pulp, and swallowed them. He pounded his fingers, too, in his haste, and yet found a moment in which to feel surprise at the fact that his fingers did not hurt much when caught under the descending rock.

Came frightful days of snow and rain. He did not know when he made camp, when he broke camp. He travelled in the night as much as in the day. He rested wherever he fell, crawled on whenever the dying life in him flickered up and burned less dimly. He, as a man, no longer strove. It was the life in him, unwilling to die, that drove him on. He did not suffer. His nerves had become blunted, numb, while his mind was filled with weird visions and delicious dreams.

But ever he sucked and chewed on the crushed bones of the caribou calf, the least remnants of which he had gathered up and carried with him. He crossed no more hills or divides, but automatically followed a large stream which flowed through a wide and shallow valley. He did not see this stream nor this valley. He saw nothing save visions. Soul and body walked or crawled side by side, yet apart, so slender was the thread that bound them.

He awoke in his right mind, lying on his back on a rocky ledge. The sun was shining bright and warm. Afar off he heard the squawking of caribou calves. He was aware of vague memories of rain and wind and snow, but whether he had been beaten by the storm for two days or two weeks he did not know.

For some time he lay without movement, the genial sunshine pouring upon him and saturating his miserable body with its warmth. A fine day, he thought. Perhaps he could manage to locate himself. By a painful effort he rolled over on his side. Below him flowed a wide and sluggish river. Its unfamiliarity puzzled him. Slowly he followed it with his eyes, winding in wide sweeps among the bleak, bare hills, bleaker and barer and lower lying than any hills he had yet encountered. Slowly, deliberately, without excitement or more than the most casual interest, he followed the course of the strange stream towards the sky line and saw it emptying into a bright and shining sea. He was still unexcited. Most unusual, he thought, a vision or a mirage—more likely a vision, a trick of his disordered mind. He was confirmed in this by sight of a ship lying at anchor in the midst of the shining sea. He closed his eyes for a while, then opened them. Strange how the vision persisted! Yet not strange. He knew there were no seas or ships in the heart of the barren lands, just as he had known there was no cartridge in the empty rifle.

He heard a snuffle behind him—a half-choking gasp or cough. Very slowly, because of his exceeding weakness and stiffness, he rolled over on his other side. He could see nothing near at hand, but he waited patiently. Again came the snuffle and cough, and outlined between two jagged rocks not a score of feet away he made out the grey head of a wolf. The sharp ears were not pricked so sharply as he had seen them on other wolves; the eyes were bleared and bloodshot, the head seemed to droop limply and forlornly. The animal blinked continually in the sunshine. It seemed sick. As he looked it snuffled and coughed again.

This, at least, was real, he thought, and turned on the other side so that he might see the reality of the world which had been veiled from him before by the vision. But the sea still shone in the distance and the ship was plainly discernible. Was it reality, after all ? He closed his eyes for a long while and thought, and then it came to him. He had been making north by east, away from the Dease Divide and into the Coppermine Valley. This wide and sluggish river was the Coppermine. That shining sea was the Arctic Ocean. That ship was a whaler, strayed east, far east, from the mouth of the Mackenzie, and it was lying at anchor in Coronation Gulf. He remembered the Hudson Bay Company chart he had seen long ago, and it was all clear and reasonable to him.

He sat up and turned his attention to immediate affairs. He had worn through the blanket wrappings, and his feet were shapeless lumps of raw meat. His last blanket was gone. Rifle and knife were both missing. He had lost his hat somewhere, with the bunch of matches in the band, but the matches against his chest were safe and dry inside the tobacco pouch and oil paper. He looked at his watch. It marked eleven o'clock and was still running. Evidently he had kept it wound.

He was calm and collected. Though extremely weak, he had no sensation of pain. He was not hungry. The thought of food was not even pleasant to him, and whatever he did was done by his reason alone. He ripped off his pants legs to the knees and bound them about his feet. Somehow he had succeeded in retaining the tin bucket. He would have some hot water before he began what he foresaw was to be a terrible journey to the ship.

His movements were slow. He shook as with a palsy. When he started to collect dry moss, he found he could not rise to his feet. He tried again and again, then contented himself with crawling about on hands and knees. Once he crawled near to the sick wolf. The animal dragged itself reluctantly out of his way, licking its chops with a tongue which seemed hardly to have the strength to curl. The man noticed that the tongue was not the customary

84

healthy red. It was a yellowish brown and seemed coated with a rough and half-dry mucus.

After he had drunk a quart of hot water the man found he was able to stand, and even to walk as well as a dying man might be supposed to walk. Every minute or so he was compelled to rest. His steps were feeble and uncertain, just as the wolf's that trailed him were feeble and uncertain; and that night, when the shining sea was blotted out by blackness, he knew he was nearer to it by no more than four miles.

Throughout the night he heard the cough of the sick wolf, and now and then the squawking of the caribou calves. There was life all around him, but it was strong life, very much alive and well, and he knew the sick wolf clung to the sick man's trail in the hope that the man would die first. In the morning, on opening his eyes, he beheld it regarding him with a wistful and hungry stare. It stood crouched, with tail between its legs, like a miserable and woebegone dog. It shivered in the chill morning wind, and grinned dispiritedly when the man spoke to it in a voice that achieved no more than a hoarse whisper.

The sun rose brightly, and all morning the man tottered and fell towards the ship on the shining sea. The weather was perfect. It was the brief Indian Summer of the high latitudes. It might last a week. Tomorrow or next day it might be gone.

In the afternoon the man came upon a trail. It was of another man, who did not walk but who dragged himself on all fours. The man thought it might be Bill, but he thought in a dull, uninterested way. He had no curiosity. In fact, sensation and emotion had left him. He was no longer susceptible to pain. Stomach and nerves had gone to sleep. Yet the life that was in him drove him on. He was very weary, but it refused to die. It was because it refused to die that he still ate muskeg berries and minnows, drank his hot water, and kept a wary eye on the sick wolf.

He followed the trail of the other man who dragged himself

along, and soon came to the end of it—a few fresh-picked bones where the soggy moss was marked by the footpads of many wolves. He saw a squat moose-hide sack, mate to his own, which had been torn by sharp teeth. He picked it up, though its weight was almost too much for his feeble fingers. Bill had carried it to the last. Ha! ha! He would have the laugh on Bill. He would survive and carry it to the ship in the shining sea. His mirth was hoarse and ghastly, like a raven's croak, and the sick wolf joined him, howling lugubriously. The man ceased suddenly. How could he have the laugh on Bill if that were Bill; if those bones, so pinky-white and clean, were Bill?

He turned away. Well, Bill had deserted him; but he would not take the gold, nor would he suck Bill's bones. Bill would have, though, had it been the other way around, he mused as he staggered on.

He came to a pool of water. Stooping over in quest of minnows, he jerked his head back as though he had been stung. He had caught sight of his reflected face. So horrible was it that sensibility awoke long enough to be shocked. There were three minnows in the pool, which was too large to drain; and after several ineffectual attempts to catch them in the tin bucket he forbore. He was afraid, because of his great weakness, that he might fall in and drown. It was for this reason that he did not trust himself to the river astride one of the many drift logs which lined its sandspits.

That day he decreased the distance between him and the ship by three miles; the next day by two—for he was crawling now as Bill had crawled; and the end of the fifth day found the ship still seven miles away and him unable to make even a mile a day. Still the Indian Summer held on, and he continued to crawl and faint, turn and turn about; and ever the sick wolf coughed and wheezed at his heels. His knees had become raw meat like his feet, and though he padded them with the shirt from his back it was a red track he left behind him on the moss and stones. Once,

86

glancing back, he saw the wolf licking hungrily his bleeding trail, and he saw sharply what his own end might be—unless—unless he could get the wolf. Then began as grim a tragedy of existence as was ever played—a sick man that crawled, a sick wolf that limped, two creatures dragging their dying carcasses across the desolation and hunting each other's lives.

Had it been a well wolf, it would not have mattered so much to the man; but the thought of going to feed the maw of that loathsome and all but dead thing was repugnant to him. He was finicky. His mind had begun to wander again, and to be perplexed by hallucinations, while his lucid intervals grew rarer and shorter.

He was awakened once from a faint by a wheeze close in his ear. The wolf leaped lamely back, losing its footing and falling in its weakness. It was ludicrous but he was not amused. Nor was he even afraid. He was too far gone for that. But his mind was for the moment clear, and he lay and considered. The ship was no more than four miles away. He could see it quite distinctly when he rubbed the mists out of his eyes, and he could see the white sail of a small boat cutting the water of the shining sea. But he could never crawl those four miles. He knew that, and was very calm in the knowledge. He knew that he could not crawl half a mile. And yet he wanted to live. It was unreasonable that he should die after all he had undergone. Fate asked too much of him. And, dying, he declined to die. It was stark madness, perhaps but in the very grip of Death he defied Death and refused to die.

He closed his eyes and composed himself with infinite precaution. He steeled himself to keep above the suffocating languor that lapped like a rising tide through all the wells of his being. It was very like a sea, this deadly languor, that rose and rose and drowned his consciousness bit by bit. Sometimes he was all but submerged, swimming through oblivion with a faltering stroke; and again, by some strange alchemy of soul, he would find another shred of will and strike out more strongly.

Without movement he lay on his back, and he could hear, slowly drawing nearer and nearer, the wheezing intake and output of the sick wolf's breath. It drew closer, ever closer, through an infinitude of time, and he did not move. It was at his ear. The harsh dry tongue grated like sandpaper against his cheek. His hands shot out—or at least he willed them to shoot out. The fingers were curved like talons, but they closed on empty air. Swiftness and certitude require strength, and the man had not this strength.

The patience of the wolf was terrible. The man's patience was no less terrible. For half a day he lay motionless, fighting off unconsciousness and waiting for the thing that was to feed upon him and upon which he wished to feed. Sometimes the languid sea rose over him and he dreamed long dreams; but ever through it all waking and dreaming, he waited for the wheezing breath and the harsh caress of the tongue.

He did not hear the breath, and he slipped slowly from some dream to the feel of the tongue along his hand. He waited. The fangs pressed softly; the pressure increased; the wolf was exerting its last strength in an effort to sink teeth in the food for which it had waited so long. But the man had waited long, and the lacerated hand closed on the jaw. Slowly, while the wolf struggled feebly and the hand clutched feebly, the other hand crept across to a grip. Five minutes later the whole weight of the man's body was on top of the wolf. The hands had not sufficient strength to choke the wolf, but the face of the man was pressed close to the throat of the wolf and the mouth of the man was full of hair. At the end of half an hour the man was aware of a warm trickle in his throat. It was not pleasant. It was like molten lead being forced into his stomach, and it was forced by his will alone. Later the man rolled over on his back and slept.

There were some members of a scientific expedition on the whaleship *Bedford*. From the deck they remarked a strange object on the shore. It was moving down the beach toward the water. They were unable to classify it, and, being scientific men, they climbed into the whaleboat alongside and went ashore to see. And they saw something that was alive but which could hardly be called a man. It was blind, unconscious. It squirmed along the ground like some monstrous worm. Most of its efforts were ineffectual, but it was persistent, and it writhed and twisted and went ahead perhaps a score of feet an hour.

Three weeks afterward the man lay in a bunk on the whaleship *Bedford*, and with tears streaming down his wasted cheeks told who he was and what he had undergone. He also babbled incoherently of his mother, of sunny Southern California, and a home among the orange groves and flowers.

The days were not many after that when he sat at table with the scientific men and ship's officers. He gloated over the spectacle of so much food, watching it anxiously as it went into the mouths of others. With the disappearance of each mouthful an expression of deep regret came into his eyes. He was quite sane, yet he hated those men at mealtime. He was haunted by a fear that the food would not last. He inquired of the cook, the cabin boy, the captain, concerning the food stores. They reassured him countless times; but he could not believe them, and pried cunningly about the lazaretto to see with his own eyes.

It was noticed that the man was getting fat. He grew stouter with each day. The scientific men shook their heads and theorised. They limited the man at his meals, but still his girth increased and he swelled prodigiously under his shirt.

The sailors grinned. They knew. And when the scientific men set a watch on the man, they knew too. They saw him slouch for'ard after breakfast, and, like a mendicant, with outstretched palm, accost a sailor. The sailor grinned and passed him a fragment of sea biscuit. He clutched it avariciously, looked at it as a miser looks at gold, and thrust it into his shirt bosom. Similar were the donations from other grinning sailors.

The scientific men were discreet. They let him alone. But they privily examined his bunk. It was lined with hardtack; the mattress was stuffed with hardtack; every nook and cranny were filled with hardtack. Yet he was sane. He was taking precautions against another possible famine—that was all. He would recover from it, the scientific men said; and he did, ere the *Bedford's* anchor rumbled down in San Francisco Bay.

JACK LONDON

Alan Sillitoe

Alan Sillitoe was born in Nottingham, England, in 1928. In the houses of the predominantly working class district where he lived, books were not common but as a boy he managed to build up a small collection of his own, bought mainly from a nearby secondhand shop. These books were important to him because, in his own words: 'Reading was the only means of going into a world other than the one around me, one which I often found disagreeable because it was too close and sometimes too alien'. His interest in books waned, however, when he left school at fourteen to work in the Raleigh Bicycle factory; later he joined the R.A.F. as a wireless operator. At the age of twenty he was forced to spend eighteen months in hospital with tuberculosis. During this period he began to read extensively again and it marked the starting point of his own career as a writer. With the small pension he received when he was invalided from the R.A.F., he decided to travel abroad while he developed his writing.

His first novel, *Saturday Night and Sunday Morning*, won the Authors' Club Award for the best first novel of 1958. It was later made into a film, as was the title story of his second book, a collection of short stories, *The Loneliness of the Long Distance Runner*. Another collection, *The Ragman's Daughter*, was published in 1963. Most of his work is based on his intimate knowledge of working class life in the industrial suburbs. The accuracy with which he captures the atmosphere of the environment, the patterns of speech and the attitudes of this section of society can be seen clearly in 'The Other John Peel' (*Storytellers 1*) and 'The Disgrace of Jim Scarfedale' (*Storytellers 2*). Both of these stories also convey a strong feeling of 'Them and Us'—the difference between working class and middle class.

The Disgrace of Jim Scarfedale

I'M EASILY led and swung, my mind like a weather-vane when somebody wants to change it for me, but there's one sure rule I'll stick to for good, and I don't mind driving a nail head-first into a bloody long rigmarole of a story to tell you what I mean.

Jim Scarfedale.

I'll never let anybody try and tell me that you don't have to sling your hook as soon as you get to the age of fifteen. You ought to be able to do it earlier, only it's against the law, like everyone else in this poxetten land of hope and glory.

You see, you can't hang on to your mam's apron strings for ever, though it's a dead cert there's many a bloke as would like to. Jim Scarfedale was one of these. He hung on so long that in the end he couldn't get used to anything else, and when he tried to change I swear blind he didn't know the difference between an apron string and a pair of garters, though I'm sure his brand-new almost beautiful wife must have tried to drum it into his skull before she sent him whining back to his mother.

Well, I'm not going to be one of that sort. As soon as I see a way of making-off—even if I have to rob meters to feed myself—I'll take it. Instead of doing arithmetic lessons at school I glue my eyes to the atlas under my desk, planning the way I'm going to take when the time comes (with the ripped-out map folded-up in my back pocket): bike to Derby, bus to Manchester, train to

Glasgow, nicked car to Edinburgh, and hitch-hiking down to London. I can never stop looking at them maps, with their red roads and brown hills and marvellous other cities—so it's no wonder I can't add up for toffee. (Yes, I know, every city's the same when you come to weigh it up: the same hostels full of thieves all out to snatch your last bob if you give them half the chance; the same factories full of work, if you're lucky; the same mildewed backyards and houses full of silverfish and black-clocks when you suddenly switch on the light at night; but nevertheless, even though they're all the same they're different as well in dozens of ways, and nobody can deny it.)

Jim Scarfedale lived in our terrace, with his mam, in a house like our own, only it was a lot nearer the bike factory, smack next to it in fact, so that it was a marvel to me how they stuck it with all the noise you could hear. They might just as well have been inside the factory, because the racket it kicked up was killing. I went in the house once to tell Mrs. Scarfedale that Mr. Taylor at the shop wanted to see her about her week's grub order, and while I was telling her this I could hear the engines and pulleys next door in the factory thumping away, and iron-presses slamming as if they were trying to burst through the wall and set up another department at the Scarfedale's. It wouldn't surprise me a bit if it was this noise, as much as Jim's mam, that made him go the way he did.

Jim's mam was a big woman, a Tartar, a real six-footer who kept her house as clean as a new pin, and who fed Jim up to his eyeballs on steam puddings and Irish stew. She was the sort of woman as 'had a way with her'—which meant that she usually got what she wanted and knew that what she wanted was right. Her husband had coughed himself to death with consumption not long after Jim was born, and Mrs. Scarfedale had set to working at the tobacco factory to earn enough for herself and Jim. She stayed hard at it for donkey's years, and she had a struggle to make ends meet through the dole days, I will say that for her, and Jim always had some sort of suit on his back every Sunday morning—which was a bloody sight more than anybody else in the terrace had. But even though he was fed more snap than the rest of us he was a small lad, and I was as big at thirteen as he was at twenty-seven (by which time it struck me that he must have stopped growing) even though I'd been half clambed to death. The war was on then—when we in our family thought we were living in the lap of luxury because we were able to stuff ourselves on date-jam and oxo—and they didn't take Jim in the army because of his bad eyes, and his mam was glad at this because his dad had got a gob full of gas in the Great War. So Jim stayed with his mam, which I think was worse in the end than if he'd gone for a soldier and been blown to bits by the Jerries.

It wor'nt long after the war started that Jim surprised us all by getting married.

When he told his mam what he was going to do there was such ructions that we could hear them all the way up the yard. His mam hadn't even seen the girl, and that was what made it worse, she shouted. Courting on the sly like that and suddenly upping and saying he was getting married, without having mentioned a word of it before. Ungrateful, after all she'd done for him, bringing him up so well, even though he'd had no dad. Think of all the times she'd slaved for him! Think of it! Just think of it! (Jesus, you should have heard her.) Day in and day out she'd worked her fingers to the bone at that fag-packing machine, coming home at night dead to the wide yet cooking his dinners and mending his britches and cleaning his room out—it didn't bear thinking about. And now what had he gone and done, by way of thanks? (Robbed her purse? I asked myself quickly in the breathless interval; pawned the sheets and got drunk on the dough, drowned the cat, cut her window plants down with a pair of scissors?) No, he'd come home and told her he was getting married, just like that. It wasn't the getting married she minded—oh no, not that at all, of course it wasn't, because every young chap had to get married one day—so much as him not having brought the girl home before now for her to see and talk to. Why hadn't he done this? Was he ashamed of his mother? Didn't he think she was respectable enough to be seen by his young woman? Didn't he like to bring her back to his own home—you should have heard the way she said 'home': it made my blood run cold—even though it was cleaned every day from top to bottom? Was he ashamed of his house as well? Or was it the young woman he was ashamed of? Was she *that* sort? Well, it was a mystery, it was and all. And what's more it wasn't fair, it wasn't. Do you think it's fair, Jim? Do you? Ay, maybe you do, but I don't and I can't think of anybody else as would either.

She stopped shouting and thumping the table for a minute and then the waterworks began. Fair would you say it was—she sobbed her socks off—after all I've struggled and sweated getting you up for school every morning when you was little and sitting you down to porridge and bacon before you went out into the snow with your topcoat on, which was more than any of the other little rag-bags in the yard wore because their dads and mams boozed the dole money—(she said this, she really did, because I was listening from a place where I couldn't help but hear it—and I'll swear blind our dad never boozed a penny of his dole money and we were still clambed half to death on it . . .) And I think of all the times when you was badly and I fetched the doctor, she went on screaming. Think of it. But I suppose you're too self-pinnyated to think, which is what my spoiling's done for you, aren't you? Eh?

The tears stopped. I think you might have had the common decency to tell me you wanted to get married and had started courting. She didn't know how he'd managed it, that she didn't, especially when she'd kept her eyes on him so well. I shouldn't have let you go twice a week to that Co-op youth club of yourn, she shouted, suddenly realising where he'd seen his chance. That was it. By God it was, that was it. And you telling me you was playing draughts and listening to blokes talk politics! Politics! That's what they called it, was it? First thing I knew. They called it summat else in my day, and it worn't such a pretty name, either. Ay, by God. And now you've got the cheek to stand there, still with your coat on, not even offering to drop all this married business. (She hadn't given him the chance to.) Why, Jim, how could you think about getting married (tap on again) when I've been so good to you? My poor lad, hasn't even realised what it's cost me and how I've worked to keep us together all these years, ever since your poor dad died. But I'll tell you one thing, my lad (tap off, sharp, and the big finger wagging), you'd better bring her to me and let me see her, and if she ain't up to much, yer can let her go and look for somebody else, if she still feels inclined.

By God, I was all of a tremble myself when I climbed down from my perch, though I wouldn't have took it like Jim did, but would have bashed her between the eyes and slung my hook there and then. Jim was earning good money and could have gone anywhere in the country, the bloody fool.

I suppose you'll be wondering how everybody in the yard knew all about what went on in Jim's house that night, and how it is that I'm able to tell word for word what Jim's mam said to him. Well, this is how it was: with Jim's house being so near the factory there's a ledge between the factory roof and his scullery window, the thickness of a double-brick wall, and I was thin-rapped enough to squeeze myself along this and listen-in. The scullery window was open, and so was the scullery door that led to the kitchen, so I heard all as went on. And nobody in the house twigged it either. I found this place out when I was eight, when I used to go monkey-climbing all over the buildings in our yard. It'd 'ave been dead easy to burgle the Scarfedale's house, except

97

that there worn't anything much worth pinching, and except that the coppers would have jumped on me for it right away.

Well, we all knew then what went off right enough, but what surprised everybody was that Jim Scarfedale meant what he said and wasn't going to let his mam play the bully and stop him from getting married. I was on my perch the second night when sucky Jim brought his young woman to face his tub-thumping mother. She'd made him promise that much, at least.

I don't know why, but everybody in the yard expected to see some poor crumby-faced boss-eyed tart from Basford, a scruffy, half-baked, daft sort of piece that wouldn't say boo to a goose. But they got a shock. And so did I when I spied her through the scullery window. (Mrs. Scarfedale was crackers about fresh air, I will say that for her.) I'd never heard anybody talk so posh, as if she'd come straight out of an office, and it made me think that Jim hadn't lied after all when he said they'd talked about politics at the club.

'Good evening, Mrs. Scarfedale,' she said as she came in. There was a glint in her eye, and a way she had, that made me think she'd been born talking as posh as she did. I wondered what she saw in Jim, whether she'd found out unbeknown to any of us, that he'd been left some money, or was going to win the Irish Sweepstake. But no, Jim wasn't lucky enough for either, and I suppose his mam was thinking this at the same time as I was. Nobody shook hands.

'Sit down,' Jim's mam said. She turned to the girl, and looked at her properly for the first time, hard. 'I hear as your'e wanting to marry my lad?'

'That's right, Mrs. Scarfedale,' she said, taking the best chair, though sitting in it stiff and not at her ease. 'We're going to be married quite soon.' Then she tried to be more friendly, because Jim had given her the eye, like a little dog. 'My name's Phyllis Blunt. Call me Phyllis.' She looked at Jim, and Jim smiled at her because she was so nice to his mam after all. He went on smiling, as if he'd been practising all the afternoon in the lavatory mirror at the place where he worked. Phyllis smiled back, as though she'd been used to smiling like that all her life. Smiles all over the place, but it didn't mean a thing.

'What we have to do first,' Jim said, putting his foot in it, though in a nice sociable way, 'is get a ring.'

I could see the way things were going right enough. His mam suddenly went blue in the face. 'It ain't like *that* ?' she brought out. 'Is it ?'

She couldn't touch Phyllis with a barge-pole. 'I'm not pregnant, if that's what you mean.'

Mrs. Scarfedale didn't know I was chiking, but I'll bet we both thought together: Where's the catch in it, then ? though it soon dawned on me that there wasn't any catch, at least not of the sort we must have thought of. And if this had dawned on Mrs. Scarfedale at the same time as it did on me there wouldn't have been the bigger argument that night—all of them going at it worse than tigers—and perhaps poor Jim wouldn't have got married as quick as he did.

'Well,' his mother complained to our mam one day at the end of the yard about a month after they'd got spliced, 'he's made his bed, and he can lie on it, even though it turns out to be a bed of nettles, which I for one told him it was bound to be.'

Yet everybody hoped Jim would be able to keep on lying on it, because they'd always had something against such domineering strugglers as Mrs. Scarfedale. Not that everybody in our yard hadn't been a struggler—and still was—one way or another. You had to be, or just lay down and die. But Jim's mam sort of carried a placard about saying: I'm a struggler but a cut above everybody else because I'm so good at it. You could tell a mile off that she was a struggler and that was what nobody liked.

She was right about her lad though. Sod it, some people said.

Jim didn't lie on his bed for long, though his wife wasn't a bad-looking piece and I can see now that he should have stayed between those sheets for longer than he did. Inside six months he was back, and we all wondered what could have gone wrong—as we saw him walking down the yard carrying a suit-case and two paper bundles, looking as miserable as sin and wearing the good suit he'd got married in to save it getting creased in the case. Well, I said to myself, I'll be back on my perch soon to find out what happened between Jim and his posh missis. Yes, we'd all been expecting him to come back to his mam if you want to know the dead honest truth, even though we *hoped* he wouldn't, poor lad. Because in the first three months of his being married he'd hardly come to see her at all, and most people thought from this that he'd settled down a treat and that married life must be suiting him. But I knew different, for when a bloke's just got married he comes home often to see his mam and dad—if he's happy. That's only natural. But Jim stayed away, or tried to, and that showed me that his wife was helping all she could to stop him seeing his mam. After them first three months though he came home more and more often—instead of the other way round—sometimes sleeping a night, which meant that his fights with Phyllis was getting worse and worse. That last time he came he had a bandage round his napper, a trilby hat stuck on top like a lop-sided crown.

I got to my perch before Jim opened his back door, and I was able to see him come in and make out what sort of a welcome his mam gave him. She was clever, I will say that for her. If she had thought about it she could have stopped his marriage a dozen times by using a bit of craft I'll bet. There was no: 'I told you so. You should have listened to me and then everything wouldn't have happened.' No, she kissed him and mashed him a cup of tea, because she knew that if she played her cards right she could have him at home for good. You could see how glad she was—could hardly stop herself smiling—as she picked up his case and parcels and carried them upstairs to his room, meaning to make his bed while the kettle boiled, leaving him a blank ten-minute sit-down in peace which she knew was just what he wanted.

But you should have seen poor old Jim, his face wicked-badly, forty-five if he looked a day, as if he'd just been let out of a Jap prisoner-of-war camp and staring—like he was crackers—at the same patch of carpet he'd stared at when he was only a kid on his pot. He'd always had a bit of a pain screwed into his mug—born that way I should think—but now it seemed as though he'd got an invisible sledgehammer hanging all the time in front of his miserable clock ready to fall against his snout. It would have made my heart bleed if I hadn't guessed he'd been such a sodding fool, getting wed with a nice tart and then making a mess of it all.

He sat like that for a quarter of an hour, and I'll swear blind he didn't hear a single one of the homely sounds coming from upstairs, of his mam making his bed and fixing up his room, like I did. And I kept wishing she'd make haste and get done with it, but she knew what she was doing all right, dusting the mirror and polishing the pictures for her sucky lad.

Well, she came down all of a smile (trying to hide it as best she could though) and set his bread and cheese out on the table, but he didn't touch a bite, only swigged three mugs of tea straight off while she sat in her chair and looked at him as if she, anyway, would make a good supper for him.

'I'll tell you, mam,' he began as soon as she came and set herself staring at him from the other end of the table to get him blabbing just like this. 'I've been through hell in the last six months, and I never want to go through it again.'

It was like a dam breaking down. In fact the crack in a dam wall that you see on the pictures came into his forehead just like that, exactly. And once he got started there was no holding him back. 'Tell me about it then, my lad'—though there was no need for her to have said this: he was trembling like a jelly, so that I was some-

times hard put to it to know what was going on. Honest, I can't tell it all in Jim's own words because it'd break my heart; and I really did feel sorry for him as he went on and on.

'Mam,' he moaned, dipping bread and butter in his tea, a thing I'm sure he'd never been able to do with his posh missis at the table, 'she led me a dog's life. In fact a dog would have been better off in his kennel with an old bone to chew now and again than I was with her. It was all right at first, because you see, mam, she had some idea that a working bloke like myself was good and honest and all that sort of thing. I never knew whether she'd read this in a book or whether she'd known working blokes before that were different from me, but she might have read it because she had a few books in the house that I never looked at, and she never mentioned any other blokes in her life. She used to say that it was a treat to be able to marry and live with a bloke like me who used his bare hands for a living, because there weren't many blokes in the world, when you considered it, who did good hard labouring work. She said she'd die if ever she married a bloke as worked in an office and who crawled around his boss because he wanted to get on. So I thought it would go off all right, mam, honest I did, when she said nice things like this to me. It made the netting factory look better to me, and I didn't so much mind carrying bobbins from one machine to another. I was happy with her and I thought that she was happy with me. At first she made a bigger fuss of me than before we were married even, and when I came home at night she used to talk about politics and books and things, saying how the world was made for blokes like me and that we should run the world and not leave it to a lot of money-grubbing capitalist bastards who didn't know any more about it than to talk like babies week after week and get nothing done that was any good to anybody.

'But to tell you the truth, mam, I was too tired to talk politics after I'd done a hard day's graft, and then she started to ask questions, and would get ratty after a while when she began to see that I couldn't answer what she wanted to know. She asked me all sorts of things, about my bringing up, about my dad, about all the neighbours in the terrace, but I could never tell her much, anyway, not what she wanted to know, and that started a bit of trouble. At first she packed my lunches and dinners and there was always a nice hot tea and some clothes to change into waiting for me when I came home, but later on she wanted me to have a bath every night, and that caused a bit of trouble because I was too tired to have a bath and often I was too fagged out even to change my clothes. I wanted to sit in my overalls listening to the wireless and reading the paper in peace. Once when I was reading the paper and she was getting mad because I couldn't get my eyes off the football results she put a match to the bottom of the paper and I didn't know about it till the flames almost came into my face. I got a fright, I can tell you, because I thought we were still happy then. And she made a joke about it, and even went out to buy me another newspaper, so I thought it was all right and that it was only a rum joke she'd played. But not long after that when I'd got the racing on the wireless she said she couldn't stand the noise and that I should listen to something better, so she pulled the plug out and wouldn't put it back.

'Yes, she did very well by me at first, that I will say, just like you, mam, but then she grew tired of it all, and started to read books all day, and there'd be nowt on the table at tea time when I came home dead to the wide except a packet of fags and a bag of toffees. She was all loving to me at first, but then she got sarcastic and said she couldn't stand the sight of me. "Here comes the noble savage," she called out when I came home, and used longer words I didn't know the meaning of when I asked her where my tea was. "Get it yourself," she said, and one day when I picked up one of her toffees from the table she threw the poker at me. I said I was hungry, but she just told me: "Well, if you are, then crawl under the table to me and I'll give you something." Honest, mam, I can't tell you one half of what went on, because you wouldn't want to hear it.'

(Not much, I thought. I could see her as large as life licking her chops.)

'Tell me it all, my lad,' she said. 'Get if off your chest. I can see you've had a lot to put up with.'

'I did and all,' he said. 'The names she called me, mam. It made my hair stand on end. I never thought she was that sort, but I soon found out. She used to sit in front of the fire with nothing on, and when I said that she should get dressed in case a neighbour knocked at the door, she said she was only warming her meal-ticket that the noble savage had given her, and then she'd laugh, mam, in a way that made me so's I couldn't move. I had to get out when she carried on like that because I knew that if I stayed in she'd throw something and do damage.

'I don't know where she is now. She packed up and took her things, saying she never wanted to see me again, that I could chuck myself in the canal for all she cared. She used to shout a lot about going down to London and seeing some real life, so I suppose that's where she's gone. There was four pounds ten and threepence in a jam-jar on the kitchen shelf and when she'd gone that was gone as well.

'So I don't know, our mam, about anything, or what I'm going to do. I'd like to live here again with you if you'll have me. I'll pay you two quid a week regular for my board, and see you right. I can't put up with any of that any more because I can't stand it, and I don't suppose I'll ever leave home again after all that little lot of trouble. So if you'll have me back, mam, I'll be ever so glad. I'll work hard for you, that I will, and you'll never have to worry again. I'll do right by you and pay you back a bit for all the struggle you had in bringing me up. I heard at work the other day as I'm to have a ten bob rise next week, so if you let me stay I'll get a new wireless and pay the deposit on it. So let me stay, our mam, because, I tell you, I've suffered a lot.'

And the way she kissed him made me sick, so I got down from my monkey-perch.

Jim Scarfedale stayed, right enough, the great big baby. He was never happier in his life after getting the O.K. from his old woman. All his worries were over, he'd swear blind they were, even if you tried to tell him what a daft sod he was for not packing his shaving tackle and getting out, which I did try to tell him, only he thought I was cracked even more than he was himself, I suppose. His mother thought she'd got him back for good, though, and so did we all, but we were off the mark by a mile. If you weren't stone-blind you could see he was never the same old Jim after he'd been married: he got broody and never spoke to a soul, and nobody, not even his mam, could ever get out of him where he went to every night. His face went pudgy-white and his sandy mouse-hair fell out so much that he was nearly bald in six months. Even the few freckles he had went pale. He used to slink back from wherever he'd been at twelve o'clock, whether the night was winter or summer, and never a bloke would know what he got up to. And if you asked him right out loud, like as if you were cracking a bit of a joke: 'Where you been, Jim?' he'd make as if he hadn't heard a sound.

It must have been a couple of years later when the copper came up our yard one moonlight night: I saw him from my bedroom window. He turned the corner, and I dodged back before he could spot me. You're in for it now, I said to myself, ripping lead from that empty house on Buckingham Street. You should have had more sense, you daft bogger (frightened to death I was, though I don't know why now), especially when you only got three and a tanner for it from Cooky. I always said you'd end up in Borstal, and here comes the copper to get you.

Even when he went on past our house I thought it was only

because he'd got mixed up in the numbers and that he'd swing back at any minute. But no, it was the Scarfedales' door he wanted, and I'd never known a happier feeling than when I heard that rap-rap-rapping and knew that this time they hadn't come for me. Never again, I sang to myself, never again—so happy that I got the stitch—they can keep their bleeding lead.

Jim's mam screamed as soon as the copper mentioned her name. Even from where I was I heard her say: 'He's never gone and got run over, has he ?'

Then I could hear no more, but a minute later she walked up the yard with the copper, and I saw her phizzog by the lamplight, looking set hard like granite, as if she would fall down and kick the bucket if you as much as whispered a word to her. The copper had to hold her arm.

It all came out next morning—the queerest case the yard had ever known. Blokes had been put inside for burglary, deserting, setting fire to buildings, bad language, being blind drunk, grabbing hold of grown women and trying to give them what-for, not paying maintenance money, running up big debts for wirelesses and washing machines and then selling them, poaching, trespassing, driving off in cars that didn't belong to them, trying to commit suicide, attempted murder, assault and battery, snatching handbags, shoplifting, fraud, forgery, pilfering from work, bashing each other about, and all sorts of larks that didn't mean much. But Jim did something I hadn't heard about before, at least not in our yard.

He'd been at it for months as well, taking a bus four miles across town to places where nobody knew him and waiting in old dark streets near some lit-up beer-off for little girls of ten and eleven to come walking along carrying jugs to get their dads a pint in. And sucky Jim would jump out of his hiding place near pieces of waste-ground and frighten the life out of them and get up to his dirty tricks. I can't understand why he did it, I can't, I really can't, but did it he did, and got copped for it as well. He did it so often that somebody must have sprung a trap, because one hard-luck night they collared him and he was put inside for eighteen months. You should have heard the telling-off he got from the judge. I'll bet the poor sod didn't know where to put his face, though I'm sure there's many a judge that's done the same, if not worse, than Jim. 'We've got to put you in clink,' the judge said, 'not only for the good of little girls but for your own good as well. People have got to be protected from the likes of you, you dirty sod.'

After that we never saw him again in our yard, because by the time he came out his mother had got a house and a new job in Derby, so's they could settle down where nobody knew them I suppose. Jim was the only bloke in our yard that ever got a big spread in *all* the newspapers, as far as I can remember, and nobody would have thought he had it in him, though I think it was a bit like cheating, getting in on them with a thing like that.

Which is why I think nobody should hang on to his mother's apron strings for such a long time like Jim did, or they might go the same way. And that's why I look at that atlas under my desk at school instead of doing sums (up through Derbyshire and into Manchester, then up to Glasgow, across to Edinburgh, and down again to London, saying hello to mam and dad on the way) because I hate doing sums, especially when I think I can already reckon up all the money I'm ever likely to scoop from any small-time gas-meter.

ALAN SILLITOE

O. Henry

O. Henry (William Sydney Porter) was born in America in 1867. His first job was on a ranch in Texas. He then joined the staff of a newspaper and only a year later bought his own newspaper business. This proved to be a failure, however, and shortly afterwards he went to Central America. On his return to Texas, he worked for a while in a drug store; he then moved to New Orleans, where for the first time he began to concentrate on his writing. Finally he moved to New York, where he remained until his death in 1910. He died 'of a slow and wasting disease' just as he was achieving real success and recognition as a writer. Although he never wrote a novel—the nearest to one was the volume *Cabbages and Kings*—he produced over a dozen books containing some 270 stories, most of which can now be found in omnibus editions of his work.

His supreme ability to provide, often in the very last sentence of a story, a totally unexpected conclusion had a considerable influence on the development of the short story. But, unlike less talented exponents of the surprise ending, he never allowed the complications of the plot to overrule other important qualities such as convincing characterisation and atmosphere. Many modern writers shun the trick plot on the grounds that it is untrue to life. Nevertheless, it is a technique requiring considerable skill: characters and situations must be real enough for us to accept, but not so authentic that the twist at the end seems artificial. 'Jeff Peters as a Personal Magnet' (*Storytellers 1*) and 'Science of Matrimony' (*Storytellers 2*) both demonstrate how complete was O. Henry's mastery of this technique.

Science of Matrimony

'As I have told you before,' said Jeff Peters, 'I never had much confidence in the perfidiousness of woman. As partners or co-educators in the most innocent line of graft they are not trust-worthy.'

'They deserve the compliment,' said I. 'I think they are entitled to be called the honest sex.'

'Why shouldn't they be?' said Jeff. 'They've got the other sex either grafting or working overtime for 'em. They're all right in business until they get their emotions or their hair touched up too much. Then you want to have a flat-footed, heavy-breathing man with sandy whiskers, five kids and a building and loan mortgage ready as an understudy to take her desk. Now there was that widow lady that me and Andy Tucker engaged to help us in a little matrimonial agency scheme we floated out in Cairo.

'When you've got enough advertising capital—say a roll as big as the little end of a wagon tongue—there's money in matrimonial agencies. We had about $6,000 and we expected to double it in two months, which is about as long as a scheme like ours can be carried on without taking out a New Jersey charter.

'We fixed up an advertisement that read about like this:

Charming widow, beautiful, home loving, 32 years, possessing $3,000 cash and owning valuable country property, would re-marry. Would prefer a poor man with affectionate disposition to one with means, as she realises that the solid virtues are *oftenest to be found in the humble walks of life. No objection to elderly man or one of homely appearance if faithful and true and competent to manage property and invest money with judgment. Address, with particulars,*

LONELY,

Care of Peters & Tucker, agents, Cairo, Ill.

' "So far, so pernicious," says I, when we had finished the literary concoction. "And now," says I, "where is the lady ?"

'Andy gives me one of his looks of calm irritation.

' "Jeff," says he, "I thought you had lost them ideas of realism in your art. Why should there be a lady ? When they sell a lot of watered stock on Wall Street would you expect to find a mermaid in it ? What has a matrimonial ad got to do with a lady ?"

' "Now listen," says I. "You know my rule, Andy, that in all my illegitimate inroads against the legal letter of the law the article sold must be existent, visible, producible. In that way and by a careful study of city ordinances and train schedules I have kept out of all trouble with the police that a five-dollar bill and a cigar could not square. Now, to work this scheme we've got to be able to produce bodily a charming widow or its equivalent with or without the beauty, hereditaments and appurtenances set forth in the catalogue and writ of errors, or hereafter be held by a justice of the peace."

' "Well," says Andy, reconstructing his mind, "maybe it would be safer in case the post office or the peace commission should try to investigate our agency. But where," he says, "could you hope to find a widow who would waste time on a matrimonial scheme that had no matrimony in it ?"

'I told Andy that I thought I knew of the exact party. An old friend of mine, Zeke Trotter, who used to draw soda-water and teeth in a tent show, had made his wife a widow a year before by drinking some dyspepsia cure of the old doctor's instead of the liniment that he always got boozed up on. I used to stop at their house often, and I thought we could get her to work with us.

"Twas only sixty miles to the little town where she lived, so I jumped out on the I. C. and finds her in the same cottage with the same sunflowers and roosters standing on the wash-tub. Mrs. Trotter fitted our ad first-rate except, maybe, for beauty and age and property valuation. But she looked feasible and praiseworthy to the eye, and it was a kindness to Zeke's memory to give her the job.

' "Is this an honest deal you are putting on, Mr. Peters?" she asks me when I tell her what we want.

' "Mrs. Trotter," says I, "Andy Tucker and me have computed the calculation that 3,000 men in this broad and unfair country will endeavour to secure your fair hand and ostensible money and property through our advertisement. Out of that number something like thirty hundred will expect to give you in exchange, if they should win you, the carcase of a lazy and mercenary loafer, a failure in life, a swindler and contemptible fortune-seeker.

' "Me and Andy," says I, "propose to teach these preyers upon society a lesson. It was with difficulty," says I, "that me and Andy could refrain from forming a corporation under the title of the Great Moral and Millennial Malevolent Matrimonial Agency. Does that satisfy you?"

' "It does, Mr. Peters," says she. "I might have known you wouldn't have gone into anything that wasn't opprobrious. But what will my duties be? Do I have to reject personally these 3,000 ramscallions you speak of, or can I throw them out in bunches?"

' "Your job, Mrs. Trotter," says I, "will be practically a cynosure. You will live at a quiet hotel and will have no work to do. Andy and I will attend to all the correspondence and business end of it.

' "Of course," says I, "some of the more ardent and impetuous suitors who can raise the railroad fare may come to Cairo to personally press their suit or whatever fraction of a suit they may be wearing. In that case you will be probably put to the inconvenience of kicking them out face to face. We will pay you $25 per week and hotel expenses."

' "Give me five minutes," says Mrs. Trotter, "to get my powder rag and leave the front-door key with a neighbour and you can let my salary begin."

'So I conveys Mrs. Trotter to Cairo and establishes her in a family hotel far enough away from mine and Andy's quarters to be unsuspicious and available, and I tell Andy.

' "Great," says Andy. "And now that your conscience is appeased as to the tangibility and proximity of the bait, and leaving mutton aside, suppose we revenoo a noo fish."

'So, we began to insert our advertisement in newspapers covering the country far and wide. One ad was all we used. We couldn't have used more without hiring so many clerks and marcelled paraphernalia that the sound of the gum-chewing would have disturbed the Postmaster-General.

'We placed $2,000 in a bank to Mrs. Trotter's credit and gave her the book to show in case anybody might question the honesty and good faith of the agency. I knew Mrs. Trotter was square and reliable and it was safe to leave it in her name.

'With that one ad Andy and me put in twelve hours a day answering letters.

'About one hundred a day was what came in. I never knew there was so many large-hearted but indigent men in the country who were willing to acquire a charming widow and assume the burden of investing her money.

'Most of them admitted that they ran principally to whiskers and lost jobs and were misunderstood by the world, but all of 'em were sure that they were so chock-full of affection and manly qualities that the widow would be making the bargain of her life to get 'em.

'Every applicant got a reply from Peters & Tucker informing them that the widow had been deeply impressed by his straightforward and interesting letter and requesting them to write again; stating more particulars; and enclosing photograph if convenient. Peters & Tucker also informed the applicant that their fee for handing over the second letter to their fair client would be $2, enclosed therewith.

'There you see the simple beauty of the scheme. About 90 per cent. of them domestic foreign noblemen raised the price somehow and sent it in. That was all there was to it. Except that me and Andy complained an amount about being put to the trouble of slicing open them envelopes, and taking the money out.

'Some few clients called in person. We sent 'em to Mrs. Trotter and she did the rest; except for three or four who came back to strike us for car-fare. After the letters began to get in from the r.f.d. districts Andy and me were taking in about $200 a day.

'One afternoon when we were busiest and I was stuffing the two and ones into cigar boxes and Andy was whistling "No Wedding Bells for Her", a small, slick man drops in and runs his eye over the walls like he was on the trail of a lost Gainsborough painting or two. As soon as I saw him I felt a glow of pride, because we were running our business on the level.

' "I see you have quite a large mail today," says the man.

'I reached and got my hat.

' "Come on," says I. "We've been expecting you. I'll show you the goods. How was Teddy when you left Washington?"

'I took him down to the Riverview Hotel and had him shake hands with Mrs. Trotter. Then I showed him her bank book with the $2,000 to her credit.

' "It seems to be all right," says the Secret Service.

' "It is," says I. "And if you're not a married man I'll leave you to talk a while with the lady. We won't mention the two dollars."

' "Thanks," says he. "If I wasn't, I might. Good day, Mr. Peters."

'Toward the end of three months we had taken in something over $5,000, and we saw it was time to quit. We had a good many

complaints made to us; and Mrs. Trotter seemed to be tired of the job. A good many suitors had been calling to see her, and she didn't seem to like that.

'So we decides to pull out, and I goes down to Mrs. Trotter's hotel to pay her last week's salary and say farewell and get her cheque for the $2,000.

'When I got there I found her crying like a kid that don't want to go to school.

' "Now, now," says I, "what's it all about? Somebody sassed you or you getting home-sick?"

' "No, Mr. Peters," says she. "I'll tell you. You was always a friend of Zeke's, and I don't mind. Mr. Peters, I'm in love. I just love a man so hard I can't bear not to get him. He's just the ideal I've always had in mind."

' "Then take him," says I. "That is, if it's a mutual case. Does he return the sentiment according to the specifications and painfulness you have described?"

' "He does," says she. "But he's one of the gentlemen that's been coming to see me about the advertisement and he won't marry me unless I give him the $2,000. His name is William Wilkinson." And then she goes off again in the agitations and hysterics of romance.

' "Mrs. Trotter," says I, "there's no man more sympathising with a woman's affections than I am. Besides, you was once the life partner of one of my best friends. If it was left to me I'd say take this $2,000 and the man of your choice and be happy.

' "We could afford to do that, because we have cleaned up over $5,000 from these suckers that wanted to marry you. But," says I, "Andy Tucker is to be consulted.

' "He is a good man, but keen in business. He is my equal partner financially. I will talk to Andy," says I, "and see what can be done."

'I goes back to our hotel and lays the case before Andy.

' "I was expecting something like this all the time," says Andy. "You can't trust a woman to stick by you in any scheme that involves her emotions and preferences."

' "It's a sad thing, Andy," says I, "to think that we've been the cause of the breaking of a woman's heart."

' "It is," says Andy, "and I tell you what I'm willing to do, Jeff. You've always been a man of a soft and generous heart and disposition. Perhaps I've been too hard and worldly and suspicious, for once I'll meet you half-way. Go to Mrs. Trotter and tell her to draw the $2,000 from the bank and give it to this man she's infatuated with and be happy."

'I jumps up and shakes Andy's hand for five minutes, and then I goes back to Mrs. Trotter and tells her, and she cries as hard for joy as she did for sorrow.

'Two days afterwards me and Andy packed up to go.

' "Wouldn't you like to go down and meet Mrs. Trotter once before we leave?" I asks him. "She'd like mightily to know you and express her encomiums and gratitude."

' "Why, I guess not," says Andy. "I guess we'd better hurry and catch that train."

'I was strapping our capital around me in a memory belt like we always carried it, when Andy pulls a roll of large bills out of his pocket and asks me to put 'em with the rest.

' "What's this?" says I.

' "It's Mrs. Trotter's two thousand," says Andy.

' "How do you come to have it?" I asks.

' "She gave it to me," says Andy. "I've been calling on her three evenings a week for more than a month."

' "Then are you William Wilkinson?" says I.

' "I was," says Andy.

O. HENRY

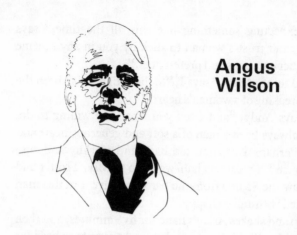

Angus Wilson

Angus Wilson was born in 1913, and spent his childhood in South Africa. A public school education in England was followed by three years at Oxford University. He then joined the staff of the British Museum. During the war he worked in the Foreign Office; afterwards he returned to the British Museum, where he had the important job of replacing the thousands of books lost in the bombing. He did not begin writing until he was thirty-three; his first two books, *The Wrong Set* and *Such Darling Dodos*, both collections of short stories, were published in 1949 and 1950 respectively. His first novel, *Hemlock and After*, appeared in 1953 and a third book of short stories, *A Bit Off the Map*, in 1957. He left the British Museum in 1955 to devote more time to writing; since 1963, however, he has combined this with teaching at the University of East Anglia. In addition to novels and short stories, he has written a number of plays and non-fictional works.

The settings and characters in his stories reflect to a large extent his own middle class background. 'Higher Standards' (*Storytellers 1*) is fairly typical of the subtle way in which he describes and analyses relationships, ruthlessly exposing human weaknesses but still retaining a degree of compassion for his subjects. 'Mummy to the Rescue' (*Storytellers 2*) also shows the same qualities but the conclusion is something of a departure from the normal structure of his stories.

Mummy to the Rescue

NURSE Ramsay was an incongruous figure in her friend Marjorie's dainty little room. Her muscular, almost masculine, arms and legs seemed to emerge uneasily from the cosy chintz-covered chair, her broad, thick-fingered hands moved cumbrously among the Venetian glass swans and crocheted silk table mats. Tonight she seemed even more like an Amazon at rest. She was half asleep after a tiring and difficult day with her charge, yet the knowledge that she must get up from her hostess's cheerful fireside and make her way home along the deserted village street through torrents of rain and against a bitter gale forced her into painful, bad tempered wakefulness. Her huge brow was puckered with lines of resentment, her lips set tight with envy of her friend's independence. It was easy enough to be dainty and sweet if you had a place of your own, but a nurse's position—neither servant nor companion —was a very different matter. She bit almost savagely into the chocolate biscuits, arranged so prettily by Marjorie in the little silver dish, and her glass of warm lemonade seemed only to add to the sourness of her mood.

'Of course, if they weren't so wealthy,' she said, 'they'd have to send her away, grand-daughter or no grand-daughter. She's got completely out of hand.'

'I suppose the old people like to have her with them,' said Marjorie in her jolly, refined voice. She licked the chocolate from her fingers, each in turn, holding them out in a babyish, captivating way of which, however, Nurse Ramsay was too cross to take any notice. 'But she *does* sound a holy terror. Poor old Joey,' for so she called Nurse Ramsay, 'you must have a time with her. They've spoilt her, that's the trouble.'

Nurse Ramsay drew her legs apart, and the heavy woollen skirt hitched above her knees, displaying the thick grey of her winter knickers, allowing a suspender to glint in the firelight.

'Spoilt,' she said in her deep voice with its Australian twang. 'I should think *so* if you *can* spoil a cracked pot. I've had many tiresome ones, but our dear Celia takes the biscuit. The tempers, the sulking you wouldn't believe, and violent too, sometimes; of course she doesn't know her own strength. So selfish with her toys—that's Mrs. Hartley's fault, "Whatever she wants, nurse," she told me, "we must give her, it's the least we can do." Well! I ask you—of course the old lady's getting a bit queer herself, that's the trouble, and the old gentleman's not much better. "You're asking for trouble," I told her, but you might as well talk to a stone wall. You should have heard the fuss the other day just because I couldn't find an old doll. "If other little girls bit and scratched when they lost their dolls," I said.'

Marjorie gave a little scream of laughter. Nurse Ramsay scowled, she was always suspicious of ridicule.

'What's funny about that?' she asked. 'Oh nothing I s'pose,' said Marjorie, 'if you're used to it, but better you than me.'

'I should think so,' said Nurse Ramsay, 'why Doctor Lardner said to me only the other day, "Nobody but you would stand it, Nurse, you must have nerves of steel." I suppose I am unusually....'

But Marjorie had closed her ears to a familiar story. She was busy wiping a chocolate stain from her pretty blue crêpe-de-chine frock, liberally soaking her little lace-bordered hanky with spittle to perform the task. Really Joey was always full of moans nowadays.

It was so very dark in the little bed and if you turned one way you would fall out and if you turned the other it was wall and you were shut in. Celia held her doll very tightly to her. She was shaking all over with fright, Nanny had pushed and scratched so because she wanted Mummy in bed with her. Nanny always tried to stop her having Mummy, because she was jealous. But you had to be careful, you had to watch your time, because however much you bit, squelching and driving the teeth into the arm-flesh, cracking the bone, they could always tie you in, as they had done before, and then even Grannie didn't help you. So she had pretended to Nanny that she was beaten, that she would do without Mummy. But Nanny did not know—Mummy was in bed. Celia pushed back the clothes and looked at the familiar blue wool by the light of the moonbeam from the window-shutter. 'It's alright when Mummy's with you, darling,' so long ago she had said that, before she went on the ship, leaving her with Granny. 'I shall be back with you before you can say Jack Robinson,' she had said, as Celia sat on the edge of the cabin trunk and wrapped her doll in the old blue cardigan. She did not come and she did not come and then she was there all the time in the blue cardigan and if she was with you it was alright. But you had to be very careful not to let them part you from Mummy's protection— they could do it by force, but only for a little because Granny wouldn't allow it; but the worst was when they tricked you into losing; Nanny had done that once and they had searched and searched, at least all of them had except Nanny, and she pretended to, but all the time you could tell from her eyes that she was wishing they would never find. The look in Nanny's eyes had enraged Celia and she had scratched until the blood ran. That had meant a bad time following, with Granny angry and Granddad's voice loud and stern, and being held into bed and little white pills. No, it was important never to be separated—so Celia took Mummy and very carefully passing the arms round her neck, she knotted them to the bedpost behind her. It was very difficult to do but at last she was satisfied that Nanny could not separate them. Then she lay back and watched the yellow moonlight from the window. Yellow was the middle light, and as they drove behind Goddard in the car—Goddard who gave the barley-sugar—with Granny smelling of flowers, they would say yellow that was the middle light, and green we move, and red we must stop, and green we move, and yellow was the middle light, and red we stop....

'It's simply a question of the money not being there,' said old Mr. Hartley, and his voice was cracked and irritable. He didn't like the business any more than his wife, and yet her refusal to comprehend financial dealings—thirty-five years before he would have found it feminine, charming—was putting him into the role of advocate, of cruel realist. He had already succumbed to a glass of port in his agitation at the whole idea and the thought of tomorrow's gout was a further irritant.

'Well, you know best, dear, of course,' his wife answered in that calm, pacifying voice which had vexed him over so many years, 'but you've often said we ought to change our lawyers, that Mr. Cartwright was a terrible old woman....'

'Yes, yes, I know,' Mr. Hartley broke in, 'Cartwright's an old fool, but he isn't responsible for taxation and this damned government. The truth is, my dear, we're living on very diminished capital and we just can't afford it.'

'Well I do my best to economise,' said Mrs. Hartley, 'but prices....'

'I know, I know,' Mr. Hartley broke in again, 'but it isn't a question of cheeseparing here and there. We've got to change our whole way of living. In the first place we've got to find somewhere cheaper and smaller to live.'

'Well, I don't know how you think we're all going to fit into a smaller house,' said his wife.

'That's just the point,' he replied, 'I don't.' He pulled his upper lip over the lower and stared into the fire, then he looked up at his wife as though he expected her to be waiting for him to say more. But she had no thought for his continuing, only a deep abhorrence and refusal of the proposal he had implied. She folded her embroidery and, getting up, she moved the pot of cyclamens from the little table by the window. 'You've been letting Nurse Ramsay get at you,' she said.

'Letting Nurse Ramsay get at me,' echoed the old man savagely, 'what nonsense you do talk, dear. Anyone would think I was a child who couldn't think for myself.'

'We're neither of us young, dear,' Mrs. Hartley said drily, 'old people *are* a bit childish, you know.'

Such flashes of realism in the even dullness of his wife's thought only irritated Mr. Hartley more.

'One thing is clear to me,' he said sharply, 'on this subject you'll never see sense. Celia gets worse and worse in her behaviour. Nurse Ramsay won't put up with it much longer and we'll never get another nurse nowadays.'

Mrs. Hartley set out the patience cards on the little table. 'Celia's always very sweet with me,' she said, 'I don't see what Nurse has to grumble at.'

'My dear,' Mr. Hartley said and his tone was tender and soothing, 'be reasonable. It can't be very pleasant you know—all these rages and the difficulty with feeding, and really she's less able to be clean in her habits than two years ago.'

The coarseness of the old man's allusion made Mrs. Hartley's hand tremble. She said nothing, however, but 'red on black.' Her silence encouraged her husband.

'I want your help, Alice, over this, can't you see that? Don't force me to act alone. Come over with me and see this place at Dagmere, you're so much better at judging these things than I am.'

Mrs. Hartley was silent for a few minutes, then, 'Very well,' she said, 'we'll drive over tomorrow.' But her daughter's voice was in her ears. 'I'm leaving her with you, Mother, I know she'll be in good hands.'

Celia was on the deck of the ship, the sun shone brightly, the gongs beat, the whistles blew and her pink hair ribbons were flying in the wind. All the stair rails were painted bright red, pillar box red like blood, and that was Celia's favourite colour. Red meant we must stop, so Celia stopped. The gentleman in the postman's suit came up to her. 'Go on,' he said, 'don't stand there gaping like a sawney.' She wanted to tell him that it was red and that she couldn't go, but the whistles and the gongs made such a noise that he couldn't hear her. 'Go on,' he cried, and he clapped his hands over her head. Such a wind blew when he clapped his hands that her hair ribbons blew off. Celia began to cry. 'A nice thing if every little girl cried when her ribbons blew away,' said Nurse Ramsay. She hoped to make Celia run after them, although it was red and that meant we must stop. But there was Granny beckoning to her and there were the hair ribbons dancing in the sunshine a little way ahead—they were two little pink dolls. So Celia ran, although it was red. And now the side of the ship had gone and great waves came up to pull her down, green and grey. 'Mummy, Mummy,' she cried, but the waves were folding over her. Mummy would not come, and suddenly there was Mummy holding out her arms to save her—Mummy all in blue. Celia ran into her mother's arms and she sobbed on her mother's bosom, she would not be lonely now, now she was safe. But Celia's Mummy's arms folded tight round her neck, tighter and tighter. 'Don't, Mummy, don't. You're hurting me,' Celia cried, and she looked up to see her mummy's eyes cruel and hard like Nurse Ramsay's. Celia began to scream and to fight, but her mummy's hands closed more and more tightly around her neck, crushing and pulping.

Nurse Ramsay heard the screams as she came up the dark drive. The battery in her torch had given out and she was feeling her way beside the wet bushes. The screams penetrated slowly into her consciousness, for she was oppressed by the memory of that humiliating scene at the Flannel Hop when Ivy had made such a fool of her in front of Ronnie Armitage. 'Really it's getting impossible,' she thought at first, 'you can't leave her alone for half an hour now without trouble.' Then suddenly something in the screams made her quicken her pace, and now she was running in panic, the branches of the rhododendron and laurel bushes catching at her like long spiky arms.

When she reached Celia's bedroom, it was already too late. No efforts of poor old Mr. Hartley or even of Goddard could bring life back to those flushed, purple cheeks, that swollen black neck. Dr. Lardner, who came shortly after, said that death was due as much to failure of the heart as to strangulation. 'She must have woken herself in struggling to free her neck from the woollen jacket,' he said, 'and the fright acted upon an already weakened heart.' It was easy to believe as one surveyed the body: the wreck of a great Britannia blonde, thirteen stone at least—she had put on weight ever since her twenty-fifth year—the round blue eyes might have fascinated had they not stared in childish idiocy, the masses of golden hair won praise had they not sprouted in tufts on the great pink cheeks, allying the poor lunatic to the animal world, marking her off from normal men and women.

Nurse Ramsay said the whole thing was a judgment. 'If they hadn't been so obstinate and had agreed to send her to a proper home she'd have been alive today,' she added. But Mrs. Hartley, who was a religious woman, offered thanks to God that night that Death had come in time to prevent her being taken away. 'It's almost as though her mother had come to help her when she was in trouble,' she thought.

ANGUS WILSON

Ray Bradbury

Ray Bradbury was born in the U.S.A., in Waukegan, Illinois, in 1920. He was educated in Los Angeles, where he still lives. He has been writing science fiction since he was twelve and has evolved a unique, richly coloured style, full of haunting, poetic images. When once asked about his writing methods, he replied: 'I write because I love writing. I'm not a thinker ... My logic is all in my emotions.' This is not to say that his work is lacking in abstract ideas. Many of his stories, particularly those set in the future, show a profound concern with the challenge presented to humanity by our ever-expanding technology. (Will these inventions improve our lives or rule them ?). 'The Murderer' (*Storytellers 2*), for example, although light-hearted in tone, still makes a serious observation on a possible development of our society and the place of the individual within it. 'A Sound of Thunder' (*Storytellers 1*) can be enjoyed simply as a good adventure yarn but it also demonstrates how delicate is the balance of our environment.

Both the above stories come from the collection *The Golden Apples of the Sun*, which contains a wide selection of Bradbury's work: there are science fiction stories with underlying social comment, tales of fantasy, and 'straight' stories set in the present. The contents of *The October Country* may be loosely described as dealing with 'horror and imagination', and their eerie mood is well illustrated by Joe Mugnani. *Farenheit 451* is set in a world where books are forbidden and where private thought and action are criminal; the rebellion of the hero, Montag, provides an exciting and thought-provoking story, which warns us, as do many of Bradbury's stories, of the dangers of submitting to the continual assaults that are made on the world of our imagination. His other books include *The Illustrated Man* (which has been made into a film), *The Day it Rained Forever*, and *The Silver Locusts*.

The Murderer

MUSIC moved with him in the white halls. He passed an office door: 'The Merry Widow Waltz'. Another door: 'Afternoon of a Faun'. A third: 'Kiss Me Again'. He turned into a cross corridor: 'The Sword Dance' buried him in cymbals, drums, pots, pans, knives, forks, thunder and tin lightning. All washed away as he hurried through an anteroom where a secretary sat nicely stunned by Beethoven's Fifth. He moved himself before her eyes like a hand; she didn't see him.

His wrist radio buzzed.

'Yes?'

'This is Lee, Dad. Don't forget about my allowance.'

'Yes, son, yes. I'm busy.'

'Just didn't want you to forget, Dad,' said the wrist radio. Tchaikovsky's 'Romeo and Juliet' swarmed about the voice and flushed into the long halls.

The psychiatrist moved in the beehive of offices, in the cross-pollination of themes, Stravinsky mating with Bach, Haydn un-successfully repulsing Rachmaninoff, Schubert slain by Duke Ellington. He nodded to the humming secretaries and the whistling doctors fresh to their morning work. At his office he checked a few papers with his stenographer, who sang under her breath, then phoned the police captain upstairs. A few minutes later a red light blinked, a voice said from the ceiling:

'Prisoner delivered to Interview Chamber Nine.'

He unlocked the chamber door, stepped in, heard the door lock behind him.

'Go away,' said the prisoner, smiling.

The psychiatrist was shocked by that smile. A very sunny, pleasant warm thing, a thing that shed bright light upon the room. Dawn among the dark hills. High noon at midnight, that smile. The blue eyes sparkled serenely above that display of self-assured dentistry.

'I'm here to help you,' said the psychiatrist, frowning. Something was wrong with the room. He had hesitated the moment he entered. He glanced around. The prisoner laughed. 'If you're wondering why it's so quiet in here, I just kicked the radio to death.'

Violent, thought the doctor.

The prisoner read his thought, smiled, put out a gentle hand. 'No, only to machines that yak-yak-yak.'

Bits of the wall radio's tubes and wires lay on the grey carpeting. Ignoring these, feeling that smile upon him like a heat lamp, the psychiatrist sat across from his patient in the unusual silence which was like the gathering of a storm.

'You're Mr. Albert Brock, who calls himself The Murderer?'

Brock nodded pleasantly. 'Before we start . . . ' He moved quietly and quickly to detach the wrist radio from the doctor's arm. He tucked it in his teeth like a walnut, gritted, heard it crack, handed it back to the appalled psychiatrist as if he had done them both a favour. 'That's better.'

The psychiatrist stared at the ruined machine. 'You're running up quite a damage bill.'

'I don't care,' smiled the patient. 'As the old song goes: "Don't Care What Happens to Me!" ' He hummed it.

The psychiatrist said : 'Shall we start ?'

'Fine. The first victim, or one of the first, was my telephone. Murder most foul. I shoved it in the kitchen Insinkerator!

Stopped the disposal unit in mid-swallow. Poor thing strangled to death. After that I shot the television set!'

The psychiatrist said, 'Mmm.'

'Fired six shots right through the cathode. Made a beautiful tinkling crash, like a dropped chandelier.'

'Nice imagery.'

'Thanks, I always dreamt of being a writer.'

'Suppose you tell me when you first began to hate the telephone.'

'It frightened me as a child. Uncle of mine called it the Ghost Machine. Voices without bodies. Scared the living hell out of me. Later in life I was never comfortable. Seemed to me a phone was an impersonal instrument. If it *felt* like it, it let your personality go through its wires. If it didn't *want* to, it just drained your personality away until what slipped through at the other end was some cold fish of a voice, all steel, copper, plastic, no warmth, no reality. It's easy to say the wrong things on telephones; the telephone changes your meaning on you. First thing you know, you've made an enemy. Then, of course, the telephone's such a *convenient* thing; it just sits there and *demands* you call someone who doesn't want to be called. Friends were always calling, calling, calling me. Hell, I hadn't any time of my own. When it wasn't the telephone it was the television, the radio, the phonograph. When it wasn't the television or radio or the phonograph it was motion pictures at the corner theatre, motion pictures projected, with commercials on low-lying cumulus clouds. It doesn't rain rain any more, it rains soapsuds. When it wasn't High-Fly Cloud advertisements, it was music by Mozzek in every restaurant; music and commercials on the buses I rode to work. When it wasn't music, it was inter-office communications, and my horror chamber of a radio wrist watch on which my friends and my wife phoned every five minutes. What is there about such "conveniences" that makes them so *temptingly* convenient ? The average man thinks, Here I am, time on my hands, and there on my wrist is a wrist telephone, so why not just buzz old Joe up, eh? "Hello, he*llo*!" I love my friends, my wife, humanity, very much, but when one minute my wife calls to say, "Where are you *now*, dear?" and a friend calls and says, "Got the best off-colour joke to tell you. Seems there was a guy——" And a stranger calls and cries out, "This is the Find-Fax Poll. What gum are you chewing at this very *instant*?" Well!'

'How did you feel during the week?'

'The fuse lit. On the edge of the cliff. That same afternoon I did what I did at the office.'

'Which was?'

'I poured a paper cup of water into the intercommunications system.'

The psychiatrist wrote on his pad.

'And the system shorted?'

'Beautifully! The Fourth of July on wheels! My God, steno-graphers ran around looking *lost*! What an uproar!'

'Felt better temporarily, eh?'

'Fine! Then I got the idea at noon of stomping my wrist radio on the sidewalk. A shrill voice was just yelling out of it at me, "This is People's Poll Number Nine. What did you eat for lunch?" when I kicked the Jesus out of the wrist radio!'

'Felt even *better*, eh?'

'It grew on me!' Brock rubbed his hands together. 'Why didn't I start a solitary revolution, deliver man from certain "con-veniences?" "Convenient for who?" I cried. Convenient for friends: "Hey, Al, thought I'd call you from the locker room out here at Green Hills. Just made a sockdolager hole in one! A hole in one, Al! A *beautiful* day. Having a shot of whisky now. Thought you'd want to know, Al!" Convenient for my office, so when I'm in the field with my radio car there's no moment when I'm not in touch. In *touch*! *There's* a slimy phrase. Touch, hell. *Gripped*!

Pawed, rather. Mauled and massaged and pounded by FM voices. You can't leave your car without checking in: "Have stopped to visit gas-station men's room." "Okay, Brock, step on it!" "Brock, what *took* you so long?" "Sorry, sir." "Watch it next time, Brock." "Yes, sir!" So, do you know what I did, Doctor? I bought a quart of French chocolate ice cream and spooned it into the car radio transmitter.'

'Was there any *special* reason for selecting French chocolate ice cream to spoon into the broadcasting unit?'

Brock thought about it and smiled. 'It's my favourite flavour.'

'Oh,' said the doctor.

'I figured, hell, what's good enough for me is good enough for the radio transmitter.'

'What made you think of spooning *ice cream* into the radio?'

'It was a hot day.'

The doctor paused.

'And what happened next?'

'Silence happened next. God, it was *beautiful*. That car radio cackling all day, Brock go here, Brock go there, Brock check in, Brock check out, okay Brock, hour lunch, lunch over, Brock, Brock, Brock. Well, that silence was like putting ice cream in my ears.'

'You seem to like ice cream a lot.'

'I just rode around feeling of the silence. It's a big bolt of the nicest, softest flannel ever made. Silence. A whole hour of it. I just sat in my car, smiling, feeling of that flannel with my ears. I felt *drunk* with Freedom!'

'Go on.'

'Then I got the idea of the portable diathermy machine. I rented one, took it on the bus going home that night. There sat all the tired commuters with their wrist radios, talking to their wives, saying, "Now I'm at Forty-third, now I'm at Forty-fourth, here I am at Forty-ninth, now turning at Sixty-first." One husband cursing, "Well, get *out* of that bar, damn it, and get home and get dinner started, I'm at Seventieth!" And the transit-system radio playing "Tales from the Vienna Woods", a canary singing words about a first-rate wheat cereal. Then—I switched on my diathermy! Static! Interference! All wives cut off from husbands grousing about a hard day at the office. All husbands cut off from wives who had just seen their children break a window! The "Vienna Woods" chopped down, the canary mangled! *Silence!* A terrible, unexpected silence. The bus inhabitants faced with having to converse with each other. Panic! Sheer, animal panic!'

'The police seized you?'

'The bus *had* to stop. After all, the music *was* being scrambled, husbands and wives *were* out of touch with reality. Pandemonium, riot, and chaos. Squirrels chattering in cages! A trouble unit arrived, triangulated on me instantly, had me reprimanded, fined, and home, minus my diathermy machine, in jig time.'

'Mr. Brock, may I suggest that so far your whole pattern here is not very—practical? If you didn't like transit radios or office radios or car business radios, why didn't you join a fraternity of radio haters, start petitions, get legal and constitutional rulings? After all, this *is* a democracy.'

'And I,' said Brock, 'am that thing best called a minority. I *did* join fraternities, picket, pass petitions, take it to court. Year after year I protested. Everyone laughed. Everyone else *loved* bus radios and commercials. *I* was out of step.'

'Then you should have taken it like a good soldier, don't you think? The majority rules.'

'But they went too far. If a little music and "keeping in touch" was charming, they figured a lot would be ten times as charming. I went *wild!* I got home to find my wife hysterical. *Why!* Because she had been completely out of touch with me for half a day. Remember, I did a dance on my wrist radio? Well, that night I laid plans to murder my house.'

'Are you *sure* that's how you want me to write it down ?'

'That's semantically accurate. Kill it dead. It's one of those talking, singing, humming, weather-reporting, poetry-reading, novel-reciting, jingle-jangling, rockaby-crooning-when-you-go-to-bed houses. A house that screams opera to you in the shower and teaches you Spanish in your sleep. One of those blathering caves where all kinds of electronic Oracles make you feel a trifle larger than a thimble, with stoves that say, "I'm apricot pie, and I'm *done*," or "I'm prime roast beef, so *baste* me!" and other nursery gibberish like that. With beds that rock you to sleep and *shake* you awake. A house that *barely* tolerates humans, I tell you. A front door that barks: "You've mud on your feet, sir!" And an electronic vacuum hound that snuffles around after you from room to room, inhaling every fingernail or ash you drop. Jesus God, *I* say, Jesus God!'

'Quietly,' suggested the psychiatrist.

'Remember that Gilbert and Sullivan song—"I've Got It on My List, It Never Will Be Missed" ? All night I listed grievances. Next morning early I bought a pistol. I *purposely* muddied my feet. I stood at our front door. The front door shrilled, "Dirty feet, muddy feet! Wipe your feet! Please be *neat !*" I shot the damn thing in its keyhole! I ran to the kitchen, where the stove was just whining. "Turn me *over !*" In the middle of a mechanical omelet I did the stove to death. Oh, how it sizzled and screamed, "I'm *shorted !*" Then the telephone rang like a spoiled brat. I shoved it down the Insinkerator. I must state here and now I have *nothing* whatever against the Insinkerator; it was an innocent bystander. I feel sorry for it now, a practical device indeed, which never said a word, purred like a sleepy lion most of the time, and digested our leftovers. I'll have it restored. Then I went in and shot the televisor, that insidious beast, that Medusa, which freezes a billion people to stone every night, staring fixedly, that Siren which called and sang and promised so much and gave, after all, so little, but myself always going back, going back, hoping and waiting until—bang! Like a headless turkey, gobbling, my wife whooped out the front door. The police came. Here I *am!*'

He sat back happily and lit a cigarette.

'And did you realise, in committing these crimes, that the wrist radio, the broadcasting transmitter, the phone, the bus radio, the office intercoms, all were rented or were someone else's property?'

'I would do it all over again, so help me God.'

The psychiatrist sat there in the sunshine of that beatific smile.

'You don't want any further help from the Office of Mental Health? You're ready to take the consequences?'

'This is only the beginning,' said Mr. Brock. 'I'm the vanguard of the small public which is tired of noise and being taken advantage of and pushed around and yelled at, every moment music, every moment in touch with some voice somewhere, do this, do that, quick, quick, now here, now there. You'll *see*. The revolt begins. My name will go down in history!'

'Mmm.' The psychiatrist seemed to be thinking.

'It'll take time, of course. It was all so enchanting at first. The very *idea* of these things, the practical uses, was wonderful. They were almost toys, to be played with, but the people got too involved, went too far, and got wrapped up in a pattern of social behaviour and couldn't get out, couldn't admit they were *in*, even. So they rationalised their nerves as something else. "Our modern age," they said. "Conditions," they said, "High-strung," they said. But mark my words, the seed has been sown. I got world-wide coverage on TV, radio, films; *there's* an irony for you. That was five days ago. A billion people know about me. Check your financial columns. Any day now. Maybe today. Watch for a sudden spurt, a rise in sales for French chocolate ice cream!'

'I see,' said the psychiatrist.

'Can I go back to my nice private cell now, where I can be alone and quiet for six months?'

'Yes,' said the psychiatrist quietly.

'Don't worry about me,' said Mr. Brock, rising. 'I'm just going to sit around for a long time stuffing that nice soft bolt of quiet material in both ears.'

'Mmm,' said the psychiatrist, going to the door.

'Cheers,' said Mr. Brock.

'Yes,' said the psychiatrist.

He pressed a code signal on a hidden button, the door opened, he stepped out, the door shut and locked. Alone, he moved in the offices and corridors. The first twenty yards of his walk were accompanied by 'Tambourine Chinois'. Then it was 'Tzigane', Bach's Passacaglia and Fugue in something Minor, 'Tiger Rag', 'Love Is Like a Cigarette'. He took his broken wrist radio from his pocket like a dead praying mantis. He turned in at his office. A bell sounded; a voice came out of the ceiling, 'Doctor?'

'Just finished with Brock,' said the psychiatrist.

'Diagnosis?'

'Seems completely disorientated, but convivial. Refuses to accept the simplest realities of his environment and work *with* them.'

'Prognosis?'

'Indefinite. Left him enjoying a piece of invisible material.'

Three phones rang. A duplicate wrist radio in his desk drawer buzzed like a wounded grasshopper. The intercom flashed a pink light and click-clicked. Three phones rang. The drawer buzzed. Music blew through the open door. The psychiatrist, humming quietly, fitted the new wrist radio to his wrist, flipped the intercom, talked a moment, picked up one telephone, talked, picked up another telephone, talked, picked up the third telephone, talked, touched the wrist-radio button, talked calmly and quietly, his face cool and serene, in the middle of the music and the lights flashing, the two phones ringing again, and his hands moving, and his wrist radio buzzing, and the intercoms talking, and voices speaking from the ceiling. And he went on quietly this way through the remainder of a cool, air-conditioned, and long afternoon; telephone, wrist radio, intercom, telephone, wrist radio, intercom, telephone, wrist radio, intercom, telephone, wrist radio, intercom, telephone, wrist radio, intercom, telephone, wrist radio . . . .

RAY BRADBURY

Guy de Maupassant

Guy de Maupassant was born in 1850 in the Norman château of Miromesnil. The parting of his parents when he was eleven made a lasting impression on him and strongly influenced his writing. Following the break-up of the marriage, his mother turned for advice to her friend Gustave Flaubert, the well-known French novelist, who later played a leading part in Maupassant's literary career. After a short spell as a soldier in the Franco-German War, Maupassant was employed from 1872 to 1880 as a clerk in the Civil Service. During this time he practised the craft of writing and regularly took his work to Flaubert for comment and correction. In 1880 he had an audacious tale about the Franco-German War, 'Boule de Suif', published in a composite volume of short stories. This brought him immediate success; he was able to earn his living by writing and became one of the most popular and highly paid of French authors. Towards the end of his life he became insane; he died in Paris in 1893.

He is best known for his numerous short stories, which often exposed the pretentiousness of the middle classes and the lower reaches of bureaucracy, e.g. 'The Necklace' (*Storytellers 1*); others dealt with the cunning and traditional meanness of Norman peasants, e.g. 'The Devil' (*Storytellers 2*); episodes in the Franco-German War also provided him with a rich source of material. His style was detached; the tone was cynical; and the stories themselves often had a surprise ending. His superb craftsmanship, verging on slickness, has caused him to be described as 'the virtual inventor of the commercial short story'. 'En Famille', 'The Rendezvous' and 'The Umbrella' are three other well-known and characteristic stories.

The Devil

THE peasant stood facing the doctor across the dying woman's bed. The old woman, calm, resigned, quite conscious, looked at the two men and listened to their words. She was going to die; she made no complaint, her time was come; she was ninety-two years old.

The July sun poured through the window and the open door, its blazing warmth falling over the floor of brown earth, its surface worn into gentle undulating hollows by the sabots of four generations of countrymen. Smells of the fields came borne on the scorching breeze, smells of grass, corn, and leaves burned up in the blaze of the noon. The grass-hoppers kept up their ceaseless crying, filling the country-side with a thin, crackling noise like the noise of the wooden crickets children buy at fairs.

The doctor, raising his voice, said:

'Honoré, you can't leave your mother all alone in this state. She will die any moment.'

And the peasant repeated dejectedly:

'But I've got to get my corn in: it's been lying too long. The weather's just right, I tell you. What d'you say, Mother?'

And the dying old woman, still in the grip of the Norman avarice, said 'Yes' with eyes and face, and gave her son leave to get his corn in and to leave her to die alone.

But the doctor grew angry and, stamping his foot, said:

'You're nothing but a brute, do you hear! And I'll not let you do it, do you hear that! If you must get your wheat today of all days, go and fetch the Rapet woman, I say, and make her look after your mother. I insist on it, do you hear! And if you don't obey me, I'll leave you to die like a dog when it's your turn to be ill, do you hear?'

The peasant, a tall, lean man, slow of gesture, tortured by indecision, between fear of the doctor and the ferocious passion of the miser, hesitated, calculated, and stammered:

'What'll she want, the Rapet woman, for looking after her?'

'How do I know?' the doctor cried. 'It depends on the length of time you want her. Arrange it with her, dammit. But I want her to be here in an hour's time, do you hear?'

The man made up his mind:

'I'm going, I'm going; don't get angry, doctor.'

The doctor took himself off, calling:

'Now you know, mind what you're about, for I stand no nonsense when I'm angry.'

As soon as he was alone, the peasant turned to his mother, and said resignedly:

'I'm going t'get the Rapet woman, seeing t'man says so. Don't worry yourself while I'm gone.'

And he went out too.

The Rapet woman, an old washerwoman, looked after the dead and dying of the village and the district. Then, as soon as she had sewn her clients into the sheet which they can never throw off, she went home and took up the iron with which she smoothed the garments of the living. Wrinkled like a last year's apple, malicious, jealous, greedy with a greed passing belief, bent in two as if her loins had been broken by the ceaseless movement of the iron she pushed over the clothes, one might have thought she had a monstrous, cynical love for death-throes. She never talked of anything but the persons she had seen die and of all the kinds of death at which she had been present, and she talked about them with a wealth of minute details (which were always the same) as a hunter talks about his bags.

When Honoré Bontemps entered her house he found her getting blue water ready for the village women's handkerchiefs.

'Well, good evening,' he said. 'You all right, Madame Rapet?'

She turned her head to look at him:

'Same as always, same as always. What about you?'

'Oh, I'm getting on fine, I am, but mother's not.'

'Your mother?'

'Yes, my mother.'

'What's the matter with your mother?'

'She's going to turn her toes up, she is.'

The old woman drew her hands out of the water: bluish transparent drops rolled to the tips of her fingers and fell back into the bucket.

She asked with a sudden sympathy:

'She's as bad as that, is she?'

'T'doctor says she'll not last through the afternoon.'

'She must be bad, then.'

Honoré hesitated. He considered various ways of approaching the proposal he meditated. But, finding none of them satisfactory, he broke out suddenly:

'How much d'you want to look after her for me until she's gone? You know I'm not rich. I can't even pay for so much as a servant. That's what has brought her to this pass, my poor mother, overmuch worrying, overmuch hard work. She worked like ten men, in spite of her ninety-two years. They don't make 'em like that now.'

La Rapet replied gravely: 'I've two charges, forty sous a day and three francs a night to the rich; twenty sous a day and forty a night to t'others. You can give me twenty and forty.'

But the peasant reflected. He knew his mother too well. He

knew that she was tenacious of life, vigorous, and sprung of hard stock. She might last a week in spite of the doctor's opinion.

He spoke resolutely:

'No. I'd rather you had a sum down, to do the whole job. I've got to take a risk one way and the other. The doctor says she'll go any minute. If that happens, you win—and then I lose. But if she holds out till tomorrow or for longer, I win and you lose.'

The nurse looked at the man in surprise. She had never yet treated death as a gamble. She hesitated, tempted by the thought of making a lucky bargain. Then she suspected that she was being tricked.

'I'll not say one way or the other until I've seen your mother,' she replied.

'Come on, then, and look at her.'

She dried her hands and went with him at once.

On the way not a word passed between them. She walked with a hurried step, while he stretched his great limbs as if he had a brook to cross at each stride.

The cows, lying down in the fields, overpowered by the heat, raised their heads heavily, lowing faintly as the couple passed them, as if asking for fresh grass.

As he drew near the house, Honoré murmured:

'Perhaps it's all over after all.' His unconscious wish spoke in the tones of his voice.

But the old woman was far from dead. She was lying on her back, in her wretched bed, her hands outside the purple calico counterpane, fearfully thin hands, knotted like the talons of some strange beast, or like a crab's claws, doubled up by rheumatism, fatigue and the daily toil which had been her lot. Mother Rapet went over to the bed and considered the dying woman. She felt her pulse, touched her chest and listened to her breathing, asked her a question to hear her voice in reply, then, having looked at her again for a long time, she went out, followed by Honoré. His

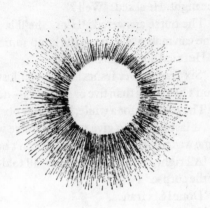

conviction was strengthened. The old woman would not last out the night. He asked: 'Well?'

The nurse answered: 'H'm. She'll last two days, p'raps three. You can make it six francs the lump sum.'

He cried out at that:

'Six francs! *Six* francs! Have you lost your wits? I swear she won't live more than five or six hours—no longer.'

They argued for a while, both very obstinate.

At last he had to give way, the nurse was at the point of going, time was passing, and his corn couldn't be got in without him.

'All right,' he said. 'Six francs, all told—including the washing of the corpse.'

'Done! Six francs.'

He went out with great strides towards his corn, which lay on the ground under the fierce sun that ripens the harvest.

The nurse went back into the house.

She had brought her sewing, for when she was tending the dying or dead, she worked unceasingly—sometimes for herself, sometimes for the family, who employed her in this double task for an extra fee.

All at once, she asked:

'I suppose you've seen the priest at any rate, Mother Bontemps?'

The old woman shook her head; and Mother Rapet, who was pious, got up with alacrity.

'Good God! Is it possible? I'll go and fetch M. le Curé.'

With that she ran to the presbytery in such haste that the urchins in the market-place, seeing her hurrying thus, thought some accident had happened.

The priest came out immediately in his surplice, preceded by a choir boy who rang a little bell to herald the passing of God through the calm, brilliant country-side. Men who were working a long way off took off their great hats and stood without moving, until the white robe disappeared behind a farm; the women who were gathering the sheaves stood upright and made the sign of the Cross; some black hens, terrified, flew along to ditches with a wild, jerky gait to a hole well known to them, where they disappeared hurriedly; a colt tethered in a field took fright at the sight of the surplice and started running round and round at the end of his string, throwing his hind leg high in the air. The choir boy in his red skirt walked quickly and the priest, with his head drooping slightly on one side and crowned with its square biretta, followed him, murmuring his prayers as he went; last of all came old Rapet, all bowed down, nearly doubled in two as though she were trying to walk and prostrate herself at the same time, her fingers clasped as in church.

Honoré, from the distance, saw them pass. He asked: 'Where'st agoing, Father?'

His labourer, quicker-witted than he, replied: 'He's taking the Sacrament to your mother, bless you.' The peasant was not at all astonished.

'That's all to the good, anyhow.'

And he went on with his work again. Mother Bontemps made her confession, received absolution and was given communion; and the priest went home again, leaving the two women alone in the stifling bedroom.

Then old Rapet began to think about the dying woman, and wondered whether she was going to last much longer.

The day was drawing in, fresher air came in in sharp gusts: a picture of Épinal, held by two pins, fluttered against the wall; the little curtains at the window, once white but yellowed now and spotted with flyblow, looked ready to take flight, to tear themselves free, as if they, like the soul of the old woman, would like to depart.

She lay there, motionless, her eyes open, seeming to await with utter indifference the death which was so close, yet so slow to

come. Her breathing, sharp now, whistled a little in the contracted throat. She would die very soon and the world would hold one woman less whom nobody would regret.

As night fell Honoré came indoors. Going up to the bed, he saw that his mother was still living and he asked: 'How are you?' just as he used to do when she was sick. Then he sent old Rapet away, telling her:

'Tomorrow at five o'clock without fail.'

She repeated:

'Tomorrow, five 'o'clock.'

She came, in fact, at daybreak. Honoré was drinking the soup he had made for himself before going out into the fields.

The nurse asked him:

'Well, has your mother gone yet?'

He replied with a malicious smile:

'She's getting on a bit better.'

Then he went out.

Old Rapet suddenly felt uneasy. She went up to the sufferer, who was lying in the same state, breathing painfully and imperceptibly, her eyes open and her clenched hands on the counterpane.

The nurse saw that this might last two days, four days, even eight days; and fear gripped her miserly heart; then she was shaken by a furious anger against this trickster who had cheated her and against this old woman who would not die.

She set to work, however, and waited, and waited, her eyes fixed on the wrinkled face of Mother Bontemps.

Honoré came back to breakfast; he seemed happy, almost jovial; then he went out again. He was certainly getting in his corn under excellent conditions.

Old Rapet was getting irritated: each minute that went by now was stolen time, stolen money. She wanted, wanted madly, to take this mulish old woman, this obstinate and pigheaded old woman, by the neck and with a little shaking make an end of the little, short breath that was stealing her time and her money.

Then she thought of the danger, and other ideas came into her head. She came up close to the bed and asked:

'Have you seen the devil yet?'

Mother Bontemps murmured:

'No.'

Then the nurse began to talk, telling her tales to terrify the feeble soul of this dying woman.

Some minutes before one breathed one's last, the devil appeared, she said, to all sick people. He had a broom in one hand, and a saucepan on his head. He made strange noises.

If you saw him, it was all over, you had only a few seconds to live. She enumerated all those in her charge to whom the devil had appeared that year: Josephine Loisel, Eulalie Ratier, Sophie Padagnan, Séraphine Grospied.

Mother Bontemps, disturbed at last, shook in her bed, waved her hands, trying to turn her head so that she could see to the farthest corner of the room.

Suddenly old Rapet disappeared from the foot of the bed. She took a sheet from the cupboard and wrapped herself in it; then she set a stew-pan on her head so that the three short curved legs stood on end like three horns. She grabbed a broom in her right hand and in her left a metal water-jug which she threw sharply in the air so that it fell down with a great noise.

It struck the floor with a terrible clatter. Then, clambering on to a chair, the nurse lifted the curtain that hung at the end of the bed and appeared, waving her arms, uttering hoarse shrieks from the bottom of the iron pot that hid her face, and with her broom threatening the old dying peasant woman, like the devil in a Punch and Judy show.

Mad with fear, her eyes wild, the dying woman made a super-human effort to get up and get away from it. She managed to get

her shoulders and chest out of bed, then she fell back with a great sigh. It was all over.

Old Rapet placidly put everything back: the broom in the corner of the cupboard, the sheet inside, the stew-pan on the stove, the water-jug on the shelf and the chair against the wall. Then with a professional gesture she closed the wide-staring eyes of the dead, placed on the bed a dish, poured into it a little of the water from the holy-water vessel, dipped in it the sprig of yew nailed on to the cupboard door and, kneeling down, began to recite fervently the prayers for the dead which she knew by heart, professionally.

When Honoré returned, at nightfall, he found her praying, and his first thought was that she had cheated him of twenty sous, for she had only spent three days and one night, which only came to five francs, instead of the six which he owed her.

MAUPASSANT

John Steinbeck

John Steinbeck was born in 1902 in Salinas, California, U.S.A. He was educated at Salinas High School and studied science at Stanford University, after which he had a variety of jobs, most of them involving manual labour. He took his native state of California as the background for most of his early short stories and novels. His first success, *Tortilla Flat* (1935)—which enabled him to become a full-time writer—was a picaresque story of Monterey *paisanas;* this was followed by *In Dubious Battle*, a grim novel about a labour strike. His concern with the depressed economic classes of the United States led him to write *The Grapes of Wrath*, an epic story of a family from the dust bowl of the West who seek work in the 'promised land' of California. This masterpiece of contemporary literature provoked much-needed reform and gained Steinbeck the Pulitzer Prize of 1940. He acted as a war correspondent overseas in 1943 and between then and his death in 1969 continued to produce a wide variety of stories. He was awarded the Nobel Prize for Literature in 1962.

Steinbeck's writing has great power: his descriptions, particularly of the landscape and of manual workers, show tremendous understanding; the pace of his stories never flags; the style is rich yet clear. Many critics, however, have called attention to over-simplification and sentimentality in his work. Traces of these faults can be detected in 'The Leader of the People' (*Storytellers 1*) and 'Breakfast' (*Storytellers 2*), but his talents are, nevertheless, much more obvious than his defects; both stories are taken from *The Long Valley* (1938). Other books that you may enjoy include *Of Mice and Men*—a story about two farm labourers, one of great strength and weak mind, who is both exploited and protected by the other; *The Pearl; Cannery Row; The Wayward Bus;* and *The Short Reign of Pippin IV*.

Breakfast

THE thing fills me with pleasure. I don't know why, I can see it in the smallest detail. I find myself recalling it again and again, each time bringing more detail out of a sunken memory, remembering brings the curious warm pleasure.

It was very early in the morning. The eastern mountains were black-blue, but behind them the light stood up faintly coloured at the mountain rims with a washed red, growing colder, greyer and darker as it went up and overhead until, at a place near the west, it merged with pure night.

And it was cold, not painfully so, but cold enough so that I rubbed my hands and shoved them deep into my pockets, and I hunched my shoulders up and scuffed my feet on the ground. Down in the valley where I was, the earth was that lavender grey of dawn. I walked along a country road and ahead of me I saw a tent that was only a little lighter grey than the ground. Beside the tent there was a flash of orange fire seeping out of the cracks of an old rusty iron stove. Grey smoke spurted out of the stubby stove-pipe, spurted up a long way before it spread out and dissipated.

I saw a young woman beside the stove, really a girl. She was dressed in a faded cotton skirt and waist. As I came close I saw that she carried a baby in a crooked arm and the baby was nursing, its head under her waist out of the cold. The mother moved about, poking the fire, shifting the rusty lids of the stove to make a greater draught, opening the oven door; and all the time the baby was nursing, but that didn't interfere with the mother's work, nor with the light quick gracefulness of her movements. There was something very precise and practiced in her movements. The orange fire flicked out of the cracks in the stove and threw dancing reflections on the tent.

I was close now and I could smell frying bacon and baking bread, the warmest, pleasantest odours I know. From the east the light grew swiftly. I came near to the stove and stretched my hands out to it and shivered all over when the warmth struck me. Then the tent flap jerked up and a young man came out and an older man followed him. They were dressed in new blue dungarees and in new dungaree coats with the brass buttons shining. They were sharp-faced men, and they looked much alike.

The younger had a dark stubble beard and the older had a grey stubble beard. Their heads and faces were wet, their hair dripped with water, and water stood out on their stiff beards and their cheeks shone with water. Together they stood looking quietly at the lightening east; they yawned together and looked at the light on the hill rims. They turned and saw me.

'Morning,' said the older man. His face was neither friendly nor unfriendly.

'Morning, sir,' I said.

'Morning,' said the young man.

The water was slowly drying on their faces. They came to the stove and warmed their hands at it.

The girl kept to her work, her face averted and her eyes on what she was doing. Her hair was tied back out of her eyes with a string and it hung down her back and swayed as she worked. She set tin cups on a big packing box, set tin plates and knives and forks out too. Then she scooped fried bacon out of the deep grease and laid it on a big tin platter, and the bacon cricked and rustled as it grew crisp. She opened the rusty oven door and took out a square pan full of high big biscuits.

When the smell of that hot bread came out, both of the men inhaled deeply. The young man said softly, 'Keerist!'

The elder man turned to me, 'Had your breakfast?'

'No.'

'Well, sit down with us, then.'

That was the signal. We went to the packing case and squatted on the ground about it. The young man asked, 'Picking cotton?'

'No.'

'We had twelve days' work so far,' the young man said.

The girl spoke from the stove. 'They even got new clothes.'

The two men looked down at their new dungarees and they both smiled a little.

The girl set out the platter of bacon, the brown high biscuits, a bowl of bacon gravy and a pot of coffee, and then she squatted down by the box too. The baby was still nursing, its head up under her waist out of the cold. I could hear the sucking noises it made.

We filled our plates, poured bacon gravy over our biscuits and sugared our coffee. The older man filled his mouth full and he chewed and chewed and swallowed. Then he said, 'God Almighty, it's good,' and he filled his mouth again.

The young man said, 'We been eating good for twelve days.'

We all ate quickly, frantically, and refilled our plates and ate quickly again until we were full and warm. The hot bitter coffee scalded our throats. We threw the last little bit with the grounds in it on the earth and refilled our cups.

There was colour in the light now, a reddish gleam that made the air seem colder. The two men faced the east and their faces were lighted by the dawn, and I looked up for a moment and saw the image of the mountain and the light coming over it reflected in the older man's eyes.

Then the two men threw the grounds from their cups on the earth and they stood up together. 'Got to get going,' the older man said.

The younger turned to me. ' 'Fyou want to pick cotton, we could maybe get you on.'

'No. I got to go along. Thanks for breakfast.'

The older man waved his hand in a negative. 'O.K. Glad to have you.' They walked away together. The air was blazing with light at the eastern skyline. And I walked away down the country road.

That's all. I know, of course, some of the reasons why it was pleasant. But there was some element of great beauty there that makes the rush of warmth when I think of it.

JOHN STEINBECK